# THE MISSING HEIRESS

## ALSO BY ROBERT GOLDSBOROUGH

### THE NERO WOLFE MYSTERIES
*Murder in E Minor*
*Death on Deadline*
*Fade to Black*
*The Bloodied Ivy*
*The Last Coincidence*
*Silver Spire*
*The Missing Chapter*
*Archie Meets Nero Wolfe*
*Murder in the Ball Park*
*Archie in the Crosshairs*
*Stop the Presses!*
*Murder, Stage Left*
*The Battered Badge*
*Death of an Art Collector*
*Archie Goes Home*
*Trouble at the Brownstone*

### THE SNAP MALEK MYSTERIES
*Three Strikes You're Dead*
*Shadow of the Bomb*
*A Death in Pilsen*
*A President in Peril*
*Terror at the Fair*
*Stairway to Nowhere & Other Stories*

# THE MISSING HEIRESS

A Nero Wolfe Mystery

*Robert Goldsborough*

MYSTERIOUSPRESS.COM

OPEN ROAD
INTEGRATED MEDIA
NEW YORK

Author photo by Colleen Berg

ISBN: 978-1-5040-7989-1

Published in 2023 by MysteriousPress.com/Open Road Integrated Media, Inc.
180 Maiden Lane
New York, NY 10038
www.openroadmedia.com

*To Suzy, Bob, Colleen, and Bonnie, for all the love and support you have shown me over the years*

# THE MISSING HEIRESS

# CHAPTER 1

It turned out to be the most exciting hockey game I had seen in years. The New York Rangers trailed almost from the opening face-off, eventually falling behind by three goals. Then they fought back, improbably scoring twice in the final three minutes to defeat Toronto, the team that would go on to win the Stanley Cup during that post–World War II season.

The sold-out arena erupted—everyone, that is, except Lily Rowan, who seemed to be elsewhere. As we made our way out of Madison Square Garden with the still-excited crowd and headed for a bar down the street, Lily confirmed what I had felt all evening: her mind was far from the ice rink. After we had settled into a quiet booth at the rear of the bar, I turned to her.

"My dear, you have been worlds away tonight. First at Rusterman's, where you seemed to find little joy in the superb veal cutlets, normally a favorite of yours. Then at the game, where you are usually among the most enthusiastic fans in the Garden, you sat on your hands, despite how exciting the action on the ice was. Care to unburden yourself to your old uncle Archie?"

"Uncle Archie, is it now?" she said. "Funny, I have never thought of our relationship as uncle and niece."

"Okay, neither have I, obviously. It was just my feeble attempt at humor, which clearly didn't strike home, judging by your expression. Seriously, what is bothering you?"

"Oh, Escamillo, you know how I hate to burden you with my problems. You always have so many challenges of your own, trying to help Nero Wolfe solve his cases."

"*Trying to help* is the operative phrase, I'm afraid. You know very well that Wolfe does all the solving, while I am just his spear-carrier. But let us get back to you. Why the glum expression tonight?"

Lily let out an extended sigh. "You have met Maureen Carr, and more than once."

"I have indeed, and what an adorable creature she is, as well as brainy and charming. Mark me down as impressed."

"I can't quarrel with your assessment. And she has been among my best friends over the years. However, something has happened . . ."

"Go on."

"As you know, two weekends ago, I was at my place up in Katonah with our women's group, a dozen or so of us meeting as we do for three or four days every March to talk about projects we are working on. Maureen was supposed to be there, as usual, but she never showed up, and in the days since, she hasn't answered her phone to me or anyone else, and not one of her friends has heard from her, which is highly unusual. All of us are very concerned."

Here, I must break into the narrative to tell you about Lily Rowan. She is my good—make that *very* good—friend, and I have known her since that day years ago when, on a job with Nero Wolfe in rural Upstate New York, a bull charged at me in a field, and I leaped over a fence to avoid him, landing on my rear end and losing my dignity in the process.

A lovely young woman in a yellow shirt and slacks leaned on the fence and clapped her hands, saying "Beautiful, Escamillo! Do it again!" That was Lily. And Escamillo, a name she has tagged me with ever since, is a toreador in the opera *Carmen*.*

Lily is very rich, having inherited millions from her father, an Irish immigrant who built much of New York City's current sewer system. She also is lazy, by her own definition, although I strongly dispute that definition. She does not have—or need—a salaried job, but she is actively involved in numerous good works, to which she gives unstintingly both of her time and her funds.

And that "women's group" to which she referred is not some gathering of idle dilettantes, but rather a loose-knit organization of volunteers committed to the financing and the betterment of orphanages, food pantries, havens for battered wives, and improved working conditions for women, among other projects. Their annual meetings at Lily's Katonah estate north of New York are to compare notes and plan strategies for the year ahead.

Lily lives in a spacious duplex penthouse in Midtown Manhattan, where she throws lavish parties, many of them benefiting one or more of the causes she supports. I often serve as a bartender at these soirees. When she is not involved in good works, Lily and I can be seen at hockey or baseball games, the opera or a Broadway play, or dancing at the Hotel Churchill. And just to keep things straight, when she and I are out on the

---

* From *Some Buried Caesar* by Rex Stout (1939)

town, I foot the bill. Now, back to that bar near Madison Square Garden.

"Tell me more about Maureen," I asked as we were served our drinks.

"She is within a year or two of my age and has been divorced for, oh . . . probably eight years now. She got a good settlement, so she says, although she has money of her own from an inheritance. Her late father ran a steel company in Pennsylvania and put her through Radcliffe, where she got a degree."

"Was her breakup amicable?"

Lily lifted her shoulders and let them drop slowly. "I suppose you could say that. Her ex-husband, Larry Corcoran, whom I don't believe you ever met, has remarried. His flirtation with the woman who eventually became his second wife probably was the reason for Maureen's breakup with him."

"Uh-huh. An age-old story. How long has it been since any of your group has been in touch with her?"

"Probably more than two weeks now, at least as far as I know. Among us, we have been talking a lot about Maureen, and we all are totally puzzled—and worried."

"Well, there's no question that she's got plenty of green stuff. Maybe she took off for a warmer climate—the Caribbean, Hawaii, or maybe even the South of France."

"Not likely, not at all," Lily said, "and unlike the rest of us, she does not have a vacation home she can go to. Something serious must have happened. Maureen has never before missed one of our Katonah gatherings, and if she's ever had to cancel for some reason, she lets me know. She is extremely responsible and conscientious."

"What about relatives? She must have some. Maybe she's gone to stay with one of them. Perhaps there has been some sort of family emergency that she's gone to help out with."

"For one thing, Maureen is almost an only child, and both her parents are long dead. It's a situation not different from my own. And now that I think about it, I don't ever recall her talking about any aunts, uncles, cousins."

"What do you mean by *almost* an only child?" I asked.

"Sorry, I did not phrase that well. Maureen does have a half brother, Everett, whom I have never met. They are not at all close, and in all the time I have known her, she has barely mentioned him."

"Bad blood?"

"I don't think so. It's more a case of having little or nothing in common. From what little I have been able to learn, Everett is quite a bit older than Maureen and is the son of her father and his first wife."

"Any idea where Everett lives?"

Lily bit her lower lip, as if in thought. "I think she once said something about him being in the New York area, but she was pretty vague, perhaps on purpose. Or maybe she didn't know. She seems to feel that he has led something of an aimless life."

"Hmm. I assume that as an offspring of a steel baron, he ended up with at least a healthy chunk of his father's estate."

"I agree with your assumption. The only other thing I remember Maureen mentioning about him was that he tended to be careless with money."

"Those who have it don't always use it well," I remarked.

"That might well be the case with this prodigal brother," Lily said.

"I should know where Maureen lives, although I'm not sure if you have ever mentioned it."

"I may not have. She has a duplex on Park Avenue up in the Sixties. It's a lavish place."

"Given your own abode, the fact that you call another apartment 'lavish' gets my attention."

"I am not exaggerating, Archie. It is a showpiece."

"Have you or any other friends of Miss Carr been at that 'showpiece' since she dropped out of sight?"

"Not that I'm aware of, although I did get the telephone number of her maid, Sofia, and called her at home. She sounded baffled as to where Maureen might have gone. 'Miss Carr said nothing to me about going away, Miss Rowan. I do not know what to think,' Sofia told me.

"You know I don't like to be a busybody; it is not my style and never has been," Lily said. "But darn it, Archie, I just can't figure out what to do, and I know something has got to be wrong."

When she refers to me as "Archie" rather than that operatic bullfighter, as she has during this conversation, I know that she's really upset and is indirectly asking for help. "Can I assume this Sofia has a key to Maureen's Park Avenue duplex?" I posed.

"She must," Lily said, "because even when Maureen is out of town, she goes there to dust and make sure things are in order for her employer's return. Are you suggesting we should get the key and take a look around?"

"As usual, you read me like a book," I said. "Do you also know where the maid lives?"

"Up in Morningside Heights, somewhere just off Broadway, I think. Maureen mentioned it once."

"Do you know Sofia's last name?"

"I don't, but maybe one of the other girls in our group does. We have all been up to Maureen's, of course, for parties and meetings, and Sofia has often been there, serving us drinks and food. I'll ask around. You think we should go to the duplex and take a look, don't you?"

"Don't you?" I countered.

Lily frowned. "I . . . well, I guess so."

"You seem unsure."

"Somehow, I would feel like a snoop going through Maureen's home."

"Now you know how I feel when I'm searching somebody's place."

"But that doesn't really make you a snoop, at least by my definition. You are at work as a private detective, which is an honorable profession."

"Tell that to our old friend Inspector Cramer sometime and be prepared for a horse laugh. Look, you have already told me how worried you are about Maureen Carr. I think that overrides any feelings you might have about being a nosy parker."

"All right, I see your point. As you so often like to say, 'I am on the case.' I'll call Sofia again, and see if we can get a key to Maureen's place from her."

# CHAPTER 2

I was in the office after breakfast the next morning when Lily rang. "I got hold of Sofia, and I told her I wanted to get the key to Maureen's duplex. She gave me her address and said I could come over anytime. But she felt that she should be present when we go to Maureen's."

"Protecting her employer's property, no doubt."

"Perhaps. Like us, she seems to be worried. She told me Maureen had never left town before without telling her where she was going and when she'd return."

I took a sip of coffee before answering. "Did you tell her I would be tagging along?"

"Yes, and she said that she had no objection."

"Glad to hear it. Did you find out her last name?"

"Jurek. It sounds like it might be Czech. She does have an accent, although her English is really quite good," Lily said.

"More likely she's Polish," I said. "She is probably one of the many Europeans who have come over here in the couple of years since the end of the war. I will pick you up in front of your building in . . . say, forty minutes, how does that sound?"

"Well . . . yes, okay," Lily replied. She still sounded uncomfortable about our undertaking.

I left a note on Wolfe's desk, telling him I would be out most of the morning. We had no pressing cases, so he had no urgent need for me at the moment, as I had already typed up his correspondence from yesterday and left it on his desk for signing.

In fact, life in the old brownstone on West Thirty-Fifth Street near the Hudson had been downright serene recently. The bank balance was in okay shape, allowing Wolfe to indulge himself as usual with his ten thousand orchids on the roof, which he tends with his orchid nurse, Theodore Horstmann, and his books, of which he is reading three at any given time. And then, of course, there are the superb meals prepared by our live-in Fritz Brenner, which doubtless contribute to Wolfe's seventh-of-a-ton bulk.

I got the convertible from Curran Motors, a block from the brownstone, where we have garaged our cars for years. I kept the top up as a buffer against the late March winds and drove north to Lily's. She was waiting for me under the canopy of her building, wearing a beret and a scarf, with the collar of her raincoat tight around her neck.

"Hope I didn't keep you waiting long," I said as she slid gracefully into the car and gave me a kiss on the cheek.

"No, your timing was perfect. I stepped outside just thirty seconds ago."

We drove north up Broadway to where the numbered cross streets jumped into the triple digits. For those visitors to New York who confine themselves to Midtown and its theaters and stores and hotels, they likely think of Manhattan as basically flat. One notable exception is Morningside Heights up near the north end of the island, home to Columbia University, St. John the Divine Cathedral, Grant's Tomb, and . . . hills. Okay, these hills may not be impressive to someone from San Francisco, but they are rocky and with sometimes steep drop-offs, and the topography makes for some interesting vistas.

There was nothing particularly interesting, however, about the blocks just west of Broadway where Sofia Jurek lived. The area was lined with bland four- and five-story brick walk-ups. At Lily's direction, I pulled up in front of one of these and we entered the bare street-level foyer, one wall of which was lined with mailboxes and buzzers. Lily pushed the button with JUREK on the card under it.

"Yes?" came the static-filled voice. When Lily gave her name, the voice said, "Three seventeen."

We trudged up the heavily worn stairways to the third floor. Down a dimly lit corridor, a head could be seen peering out into the hallway.

"Hello, Sofia," Lily said to the petite, dark-haired woman in the doorway. "It's nice to see you."

"It is very nice to see you also, Miss Rowan," Sofia replied formally, looking at me with a questioning expression.

"This is my friend, Archie Goodwin," Lily explained as we walked into the living room that seemed too filled with furniture, but was nonetheless neat. "He will be going with us to Miss Carr's home. I will ask again as I did when we talked on the telephone earlier today: Do you have any idea where Miss Carr might have gone?"

Sofia shook her head vigorously. "I do not, not at all. Please sit down, both of you. Would you like to have some coffee? I have a pot made."

I was about to say no thanks, but Lily had other ideas. "That would be very nice," she said as our hostess hustled out of the room, presumably in the direction of the kitchen. "I have a few other questions to ask her," Lily said in a voice just above a whisper.

"That's usually my line," I semi-whispered in reply.

"Sometimes a woman is more comfortable answering questions from another woman. I hope you don't take offense."

"None taken," I replied as Sofia came in with steaming cups of coffee on a tray.

"Thank you so much," Lily said as we sat, she and I on a sofa with plaid slipcovers and our hostess in a chair facing us. "I seem to remember you telling me once that your husband works for a scrap metal company over in Brooklyn."

"That is right, Miss Rowan. He is there now."

"How long have you been married?"

Sofia rolled her eyes, as if thinking. "Almost six years, yes. I was what you call a 'war bride,'" she said, cheeks flushing.

"That is very romantic," Lily said with a smile. "So, your husband is American?"

"Stan fought in your army, yes, Miss Rowan. We met in England just after the war was ending. I was one of many from Poland who were moved to London when the fighting still went on. We were married there. My name was Kaminski then, a very Polish name. But I am a Jurek now, which is much shorter. And that is nicer, I think."

"Do you have children?"

"Not yet," Sofia said. "Stan felt we should get settled in and save some money first. But we do want to have a family."

Lily nodded. "Let me ask you about Miss Carr," she said. "Before she . . . left, did she appear to be worried or upset to you?"

"No, the last time I saw her, she did not seem to be at all unhappy."

"When was that?"

"I think two weeks ago last Wednesday. I go to Miss Carr's three times each week, sometimes more if she needs me to help when she has guests."

"On that day, did she tell you she would be taking a trip?"

"No, she said nothing about any trip to me, Miss Rowan, as I told you before."

"And what happened the next time you went to her apartment?"

"That was a Friday. Miss Carr was not there."

"Were you surprised?"

"No, she very often was not at home when I came in the morning. She is very busy, with many meetings, breakfasts, lunches."

"Yes, I know, and I am at some of those very same meetings," Lily said. "When did you become worried about her?"

"I think it was on Monday. Again, she was not home, and there was no message for me. She often left me, what do you call them . . . instructions?"

"Did you make a telephone call to anyone asking about Miss Carr?"

Again, Sofia shook her head. "Was I wrong to not tell someone?"

"No, no, not at all," Lily assured her, reaching over and lightly squeezing the young woman's arm. "Thank you so much for the coffee. I think we should go down to Miss Carr's now. Archie, be a dear and carry the cups and pot back to the kitchen."

"Oh no, no, I should do that, Miss Rowan."

"Mr. Goodwin is perfectly capable. I don't want to see him spoiled," Lily said with a laugh. Knowing my role, I put the cups, spoons, and pot on the tray and headed for the small and neat kitchen with Sofia at my side.

"You can just put everything down next to the sink, Mr. Goodwin," she said, going to the wall next to a calendar, taking a key off one of a series of hooks, and slipping it into her pocket. We returned to the living room, where Lily was putting her beret on. "You make very good coffee, Sofia," she said. "And now we all are off."

Sofia nodded, her expression somber. It was obvious she had mixed emotions about our venture. "I will get my raincoat," she said.

"You make a good detective," I whispered to Lily. "Ask a few personal questions first to make the interrogee relax, and then start in with the more probing ones."

"I hardly think I asked anything that was very probing," Lily replied. "By the way, is interrogee really a word?"

"All I can say is Nero Wolfe has used it in the past, so I rest my case. Now, let's go." As we left the apartment, Sofia's face still registered uncertainty.

The drive southeast found us in front of a brick-and-stone Park Avenue tower with a modest dark blue canopy in front. Any wealth this building contained, and there had to be plenty of it, was not reflected in its subdued exterior. As someone once said, the really rich have no need to flaunt it.

I parked in defiance of the posted regulations and we greeted the uniformed doorman, whose face had Ireland written all over it. His coat had the word *Seamus* stitched on the front, confirming his roots. "We are dear friends of Miss Carr," Lily told him with the same dazzling smile that first captivated me years ago. "And you of course know Mrs. Jurek."

"Yes, although I refer to her as Sofia," Seamus said, touching the brim of his hat, winking at the young woman, and returning Lily's smile. "I have not seen Miss Carr for some time," he said, turning serious. "Has she been away?"

"Yes, and we promised that we would look in on her place," Lily improvised, showing him the key. "I am Lily Rowan, and this is my friend Mr. Goodwin."

"I am very good with faces, and I of course recognized you, Miss Rowan, from the many times that you have been here to see Miss Carr. All of you, please go right on up."

The building had no hall man, so we breezed through the vaulted and chandeliered lobby to the automatic elevators.

"Needless to say, Maureen occupies the penthouse," Lily said to me as the three of us were smoothly carried skyward. The doors opened at the eleventh floor, and we found ourselves in a circular entrance hall, done in the *moderne* style, with indirect lighting and a black-and-white-checked tile floor that gleamed. Through an archway, I could see what probably was a living room, also high-ceilinged, although in a layout like this, it probably carried a more impressive name, maybe *salon* or *drawing room*.

"Also, needless to say, Maureen occupies all of this floor and the one above it. And that puts her at the very top," Lily informed me, gesturing toward a stairway that wound upward.

"To use your phrase, 'needless to say.' And similar to you in your own nearby aerie, I suppose she has a terrace as well."

"She does indeed. First, it's 'interrogee' and now 'aerie.' It seems to me that you're showing off." I know Lily well enough to tell when she is nervous, and when that happens, she often covers her unease with light banter, as if she doesn't have a care in the world.

Turning to Sofia, Lily said, "Where do you think we should

look first? You know this apartment far better than I do. And Mr. Goodwin has of course never been here."

The young woman had apparently overcome her reluctance at this excursion, and she seemed ready to take orders. "Wherever you suggest," she said.

"We should start with Miss Carr's bedroom. What do you think?" I addressed the question to Sofia, trying to give her some say over the proceedings.

She smiled shyly. "Yes . . . I . . . yes, if you think so." She led us down a hall with several doors and opened one at the end.

And what a boudoir it was that greeted us. A corner room twice the size of Wolfe's office had large windows that looked out upon the sprawl of Central Park to the north.

The scene within the room was impressive as well. The carpeting and furnishings were a dazzling white, and the canopied bed, with a white spread, of course, looked large enough to accommodate several people. "All that's needed here is a couple of white Corgi puppies to complete the effect," I observed.

"Now there is no need to be acerbic. This very room, and indeed the whole apartment, has been featured in two of the toniest home decor magazines," Lily said.

"I stand chagrined. By the way, you are pretty snappy with the vocabulary yourself, as in 'acerbic.'"

"I am only trying to keep pace with you."

"Noted. Sofia, do things in here appear to be in order to you?"

She nodded, looking around. "Nothing seems to be out of place, Mr. Goodwin."

"You may want to check some of the other rooms to see if you find anything that doesn't look as it should," I suggested.

Another nod, and she went out, leaving the two of us. "I get the idea that you wanted to get rid of her," Lily said, narrowing her eyes.

"Was I that obvious?"

"Oh, I suppose not, at least to anyone but me. I figure that you want to have free rein to go through Lily's private quarters, right?"

"You have found me out. I assume you've been in this part of Miss Carr's residence."

"Yes, but only a few times."

"Does she have some sort of an office?"

"Oh, she does, right through here," Lily said, opening a door on the far side of the bedroom. Referring to the room we entered as an office would be doing it an injustice. As spacious as the bedroom, it contained among other items a dark wood rolltop desk with pigeonholes that looked like it belonged to a small-town banker. Next to the desk was a wooden, three-drawer filing cabinet of the same vintage as the desk.

"These certainly don't seem to go with the rest of the decor I've seen so far," I said to Lily, gesturing to the desk and cabinet.

"Maureen told me once that these belonged to her father, the Pennsylvania steel man, and she keeps them to honor his memory, much like I have a gallery of photos of my own father from when he was building all those sewers that run under Manhattan."

"Makes sense. Now if you don't have any objection, I'm going through the desk and the files."

"I have no objection whatever. Do you need some help?"

"Yes, let's take a look at what we find together," I said as I pulled open the center desk drawer, which contained only a few recent press clippings from New York papers in a manila folder. I showed them to Lily.

"I have several of these, too," she said. "They are all items, mostly in the newspapers' society pages, about events held by some of the organizations we both are involved in. Maureen and I, along with the others in our women's circle, love to see publicity, not as much for our own egos but because we have found that these stories about our events end up drawing in new volunteers—and financial gifts, as well."

"Admirable," I said, checking the pigeonholes but finding nothing in them other than a couple of playbills from recent Broadway shows. "Tell me about Maureen's social life," I asked Lily.

"Since her divorce from Corcoran, she has gone out with probably at least a half-dozen men."

"I am not surprised. Anyone in particular she's serious about?"

"I'm not sure. Maureen doesn't talk a lot about the men she sees. You've probably run into one or more of them in gatherings at my place."

"Now that you mention it, I have. I ran into an ad man there named Eric one night. Very extroverted, hardly surprising for someone in advertising. It's easy to see how he could make a hit with the clients that the agency is trying to land."

"Yes, I've met him several times," Lily said, "tall, well dressed, and full of smiles, last name Mason, and he wears a tuxedo well. I remember running into them at the opera. I'm not sure whether he and Maureen are still an item, although they very well might be."

"After she got divorced, she returned to using her maiden name," I observed.

"Actually, Maureen never changed her last name. She is what you would call a modern—and independent—woman in that respect, meaning that she is not about to take a man's name just because she has married him."

"Hmm. What is your opinion on that subject?"

"I applaud the lady's stance."

"Good to know. . . . Well, there doesn't seem to be anything of help for us in the desk, so I'm going to tackle the filing cabinet," I said, pulling open the top drawer and taking out a batch of neatly labeled manila folders. I spread them out on a small table on the other side of the room.

"Okay, let's find out what we can," I told Lily.

"I really feel strange about this, as though I am somehow a trespasser."

"I can understand that, but what you call 'trespassing' may be the only way we have right now of learning what has happened to a very good friend of yours." She nodded her agreement, and we began wading through the file folders.

# CHAPTER 3

Maureen turned out to be very thorough in her record keeping, which did not surprise Lily, who said, "She has always been very precise and efficient in everything she does."

Her precision, admirable though it was, did nothing to help us learn anything as to her possible whereabouts. Although Maureen was a wealthy woman, she was not careless with money, and she was very meticulous in putting down every dollar she spent, from four-figure designer gowns to eight-dollar lunches, as we found in reviewing her receipts.

"You look troubled, my dear," Lily said after I had waded through the last of the folders in the filing cabinet.

"What I had hoped to find, either in the desk or in the files, was a datebook, or at least a schedule of her activities," I said.

"She probably took it with her," Lily said, but then she snapped her fingers and slapped her forehead lightly. "Of course—I have been a fool, and so have you, although you should be more ashamed than me, having searched through so many homes and offices in the past. It's back to the bedroom for us."

I followed Lily, and of course quickly realized what she was talking about. She went straight to the elegant white nightstand with an elegant lamp next to the bed and pulled open the drawer, tossing aside a black sleeping mask and a couple of bottles of pills before holding up a small book, white, of course, and looking at me from over her shoulder with what I would best describe as a triumphant smile.

"The shame is on both of us for not thinking about that nightstand right away," she said as we sat side by side on the bed and began paging through the personal journal, working backward from the last entry, which was more than two weeks ago.

That last entry, on a Thursday, was *Katonah weekend*, written in her finishing school cursive. "Well, you know that one," Lily said. "The gathering that Maureen never showed up for."

"Yeah, and everything covering the last two weeks-plus is blank."

"We flipped to the next-to-last notation, on a Wednesday: *Met Opera, Tannhäuser, L.T.* "Any ideas who this L.T. is?"

Lily thought for a second, forehead creased, and said, "It must be Lloyd Thorne. I didn't realize she had been seeing him anymore."

"What can you tell me about the man?" I asked, sliding my notebook out of a pocket.

"I met him only once, at a single mothers' benefit at my place, several months ago. You weren't there that night because you had your weekly poker game at Saul Panzer's. Thorne seemed like an amiable fellow, a patent attorney at one of the big, prestigious firms in Midtown."

"Any idea how Maureen feels about him?"

Lily shrugged. "Maureen always has been circumspect in discussing her social life. She dates a lot, which should not surprise you, especially given how impressed you seemed to be with her."

"Merely an objective observation," I replied.

"You did not seem so very objective at that Waldorf cocktail party raising money for women's shelters. You spent so much time in a corner talking to Maureen that I had to break up your tête-à-tête and remind you both to circulate."

"She was just curious about how a private detective works, and to be polite, I was telling her about some of my experiences."

"Okay, that explanation is almost plausible," she said. "Let's get back to work."

We came across a variety of appointments—hairdresser, massage, dress fitting—and meetings, some of which Lily recognized: "*BCR*, that's Breast Cancer Research, *WRO*, Women's Rights Organization. I was at that session; I remember it was right here, on Maureen's terrace."

More interesting to me were the entries that involved what appeared to be dates, with initials presumably indicating Maureen's escorts. "Here we have *Dinner at Sardi's, J.R.; Ballet, W.T.; Dinner at '21,' E.M.; Gilbert & Sullivan Operetta, C.D.*; *Knicks game at the Garden, E.M.*; *BCR Dinner, E.M.*," I told Lily. "Any idea who these guys are—or at least should I assume they're all guys?"

She allowed herself several seconds of looking skyward before her response. "I'm trying to recall which of these men I've actually met, and which ones I've only heard Maureen mention. Let's see . . . J.R., that must be Jason Reed, who is a publisher with Ferris and Reed, which specializes in history and biography, not much fiction. With his company's tastes, I'm guessing your boss has read some of their titles."

"Could be. I can't keep up with his books, given that he often goes through several in a week, and he keeps Murger's in business. That's a—"

"I know, that is a bookstore. And I've been in there. Have you?"

"Yes, but only once to pick up some books Wolfe had ordered, when I just happened to be in that neighborhood," I said. "Usually, Murger's makes deliveries to the brownstone, seeing as my boss is a very good customer of theirs. Have you met Jason Reed?"

"I have, once, at an auction benefiting children's hunger. As you would expect, given Maureen's obvious desirability, she would attract interesting men, and Jason was both interesting and charming—and not hard on the eyes."

"Sounds like he may have captivated you," I remarked.

"Oh, do you really think that it is only men—including yourself, of course—who are drawn to the opposite sex?"

"Just making an observation, that's all. Did Maureen have an extended relationship with this dashing and charming publisher?"

"Not that I am aware of," Lily said. "I did remark to her after meeting Reed that I thought he was quite impressive. I remember she acted rather blasé about the man, as though she didn't really seem to care one way or the other."

"She is hard to please, eh?"

"Maybe she sets high standards for herself. Or more likely, she was overly suspicious of all men after her husband's behavior. I am not sure she saw much of Jason Reed after that night at the auction. I don't recall her mentioning him again."

"What do you think of women who in their datebooks use only the initials of the men they're going out with?"

"What in the world is wrong with that?" Lily asked. "It's just a form of shorthand, nothing that's necessarily secretive."

"Does that mean that I am 'A.G.' in your calendar on the nights when we go out?"

"Since you insist on knowing, I always write you down as just plain 'A.'"

"I thought if you used my second initial, it might differentiate me from any Aaron, Anthony, Alan, or Algernon you might be seeing."

"Believe me, I would never, and I do mean never, date anyone named Algernon. Now, as I said before, let us go back to work before Sofia gets antsy and wonders what's taking us so long."

"Thanks for keeping me focused. What can you tell me about W.T., C.D., and E.M.?"

"That first one would be Will Talmadge, who's an interesting case," Lily said. "He inherited millions, or so it's said, from his father, who made his money in, of all things, electronic cables that run under the streets, if you can believe it."

"I can believe it. After all, your own late father, who I regret never having met, made his own fortune in the sewer business, so much of his work was also beneath the streets."

"As I've said before, you would have liked him."

"I have no doubt whatever of that. Have you met Mr. Talmadge?"

"I have, twice. The best description of him I can come up with is debonair. He is a good deal older than Maureen, dresses exceedingly well, has white hair and a matching mustache, and smokes a pipe. He was divorced years ago and has no offspring I'm aware of. He likes being seen in the company of younger women, and by all accounts, they like being around him, too."

"Does he have a job, or can he just live on the interest from family investments?"

"Probably the latter. He is a patron of the arts, and he has backed several Broadway plays, and some operas as well. And for the record, he lives in the Dakota."

"Which means he brushes shoulders with a lot of other well-known people. Any idea how Maureen feels about him?"

"I don't. As I have said, she doesn't talk a lot about the men she sees, and I don't think she has been out with Talmadge more than a few times."

"Moving right along, who, pray tell, is C.D.?"

Lily looked at the ceiling again, as if seeking inspiration. "Mm, that would be . . . Clay Dalton, whom I know very little about, other than that he comes from a family that has made its fortune in the construction business—roads, bridges, tunnels.

"I met him just once, when he was with Maureen at a benefit dinner at the Waldorf. He was a little rough around the edges but seemed to be a decent fellow. As I said, his money comes from the construction business. I didn't get the impression that there was anything serious between them, though."

"And what about E.M., the one who seems to pop up most often on our girl's dance card?" I asked. "Oh, wait. Of course, that's Eric Mason, the ad guy I met at one of your soirees. The one who was oozing confidence and personality."

"He should have a lot of self-confidence," Lily said. "Eric's with the agency Gordon and Grove and is among the top creative directors in New York. He's won both a potful of awards and has earned a big salary in the process."

"I see a pattern emerging," I said. "La Carr appears to enjoy the company of well-heeled gentlemen."

Lily raised an eyebrow at me. "If you are suggesting that she is a gold digger, I would remind you that Maureen has plenty of money of her own. The fact that she has dated well-off men probably has to do with the social circles she moves in."

"You make a good point. I do believe we now have plumbed the lady's diary for all the information that we are likely to get. I'm sure you noticed that the datebook was completely blank after the Katonah weekend. Didn't that strike you as strange, given how busy our Miss Carr normally is?"

"It did, and I think I see where you are going with this, Mr. Detective. She has planned to . . . well, go away."

"Certainly possible. What else was missing?"

She bit a lip. "I'm not sure what you're getting at."

"We found her diary of activities, all right. But no address book."

"Ah, of course, meaning she has taken it with her."

"Seems likely. Well, we have been in the boudoir long enough. Shall we see if Sofia has learned anything?"

Lily nodded her agreement and we found the maid in the pantry, where she apparently had been going through the shelves. Before either of us could ask, she replied, "I thought perhaps I might find out if Miss Carr had taken some food, either from here or the refrigerator, but everything seems as I had left it. Except, certain things had to be thrown out of the refrigerator, of course."

"Certainly," Lily said. "What about elsewhere, did everything seem to be in order?"

Sofia nodded, biting a lip. "I do not like to be a . . ."

"I know what you are about to say," Lily replied, "and I agree that this is very difficult, but we all are worried about Miss Carr. Do you think if we go through her clothes, we will be able to find what she might have taken with her?"

Sofia looked more uncomfortable than ever. "But she has so much clothing, Miss Rowan. I would not know what might be missing."

"I agree, but let us at least take a look. You might have a

better idea than I do as to what is in her wardrobe. And among her jewelry, for that matter."

Lily gave me a look indicating that I would be of no help whatever in perusing Maureen Carr's clothes closets and jewel boxes, and I wholeheartedly agreed. The two of them went one way while I headed for the living room, or whatever it was called.

I spent the next forty minutes playing at being a detective, which in this case meant moving through all the other areas in this double-decked palace. I spent the most time in an upstairs room that could pass for a library, with built-in bookshelves along one wall. And before you ask, yes, I opened every book and shook it, and nothing fell out other than one bookmark, from a copy of *Arrowsmith* by Sinclair Lewis. The pages where the bookmark had been yielded no clues.

Overall, the rooms I went through gave no indication of a sudden departure by the lady of the house. Other than very light coats of dust on tabletops, everything appeared to be neat and in place, surely a tribute to the conscientiousness of Sofia Jurek and her frequent visits to the apartment. I had just come down from upstairs when Lily and Sofia emerged into the entrance hall from the corridor leading to the bedrooms.

"Well, we struck out, to use one of your favorite baseball terms," Lily told me. "Maureen has so many clothes and so much jewelry that it is almost impossible to tell what she may have gone off with, although for what it's worth, the string of pearls she loves so much was in place. We also looked in the closet where her suitcases are kept and couldn't tell if any were missing, because neither Sofia nor I know how many pieces of luggage she had to begin with."

"A noble effort, indeed," I said. "And I regret to tell you I had no success, either. If you two agree with me, we should leave." I got no argument from either of them, and Sofia's face registered relief. We said a brief good-bye to the doorman and drove north in silence until I dropped Sofia off in front of her building in Morningside Heights.

"I am so sorry that I was not of any help," she said as she stepped out of the convertible. "So very sorry."

"We did all that we could," Lily assured her as I pulled away from the curb. After riding several blocks in silence, Lily said, "But we really haven't done all that we can."

"I am open to suggestions."

"I really should have said *I* haven't done all that I can."

"Explain yourself, Miss Rowan."

"I plan to talk to each of the men Maureen had been with socially in recent times, starting with the one most recently mentioned in her diary, Lloyd Thorne. From meeting with him, I will work backward."

"I would be happy to help," I said, meaning it.

"Oh, I know you would, but I have already taken more than enough of your time. This really is my challenge, and what I see as my responsibility. Maureen has been a friend of mine for a long time, probably my closest lady friend, and I would be remiss if I did not try to find out what is going on."

"May I make a suggestion?"

Lily smiled. "Well, of course you can; all ideas are welcome."

"I assume many of your friends have vacation homes, be they in Florida, or California, the Caribbean, or even Europe. It could be worth checking to see if Maureen might be staying at one of those retreats, since you've told me that she doesn't have a getaway place that she owns."

"An excellent thought," she said, sighing. "It seems that I have a lot on my plate right now, by choice. I am going to begin my own version of sleuthing tomorrow, and I hope to live up to your high standards, Detective Goodwin."

"I have no doubt you are ready for the challenge. Just know that I'm available if needed," I told her as we pulled up in front of her building and embraced.

# CHAPTER 4

The next morning, I parked at my desk in the office finishing my last cup of breakfast coffee when the elevator doors in the hall opened and Nero Wolfe strode into the office, right on time at 11:03. He placed a raceme of purple *miltonia* in the vase on his blotter and settled into the reinforced chair built to handle his weight.

"Good morning, Archie, did you sleep well?" he asked as he rang for beer.

"I did, the usual five hundred ten minutes. As you can see, I've stacked the morning delivery from the post office on your desk. Nothing particularly interesting."

Wolfe flipped through the pile of mostly junk mail and scowled as Fritz Brenner brought in two bottles of chilled Remmers and a stein on a tray, placed the array in front of his boss, and returned to the kitchen.

After he had taken his first healthy drink of beer, I spoke to my employer: "Miss Rowan is highly troubled at the moment."

"Indeed?" he said, eyebrows climbing halfway up his forehead. "And why would that be?"

Although Wolfe avoids the company of women whenever possible, he makes a marked exception for Lily Rowan. His affinity for her stems from their first meeting years ago when she asked if she could see his ten thousand orchids in the climate-controlled greenhouse on the roof of the brownstone. Since then he has sent her orchids from his collection every year on her birthday. And she is one of the few females who has shared dinner at his table—and on several occasions.

I proceeded to describe the Maureen Carr situation in detail, and when I had finished, Wolfe leaned back, interlacing his fingers over his middle mound. "You showed admirable restraint in stepping aside and allowing Miss Rowan to conduct her investigation unfettered," he said. "She is an independent individual and needs to be treated as such."

"I have known that about her for years," I said. "She is aware that I will be around if needed, but for now, I plan to stay on the sidelines."

Wolfe dipped his chin in what was a sign of approval for my stance. "If at any time you feel she has need for counsel, she will of course be welcome here." His remark did not surprise me, and I told him we should keep that option open.

The days passed. We had one short-lived and reasonably remunerative case, in which Wolfe, with minimal help from me, was able to identify the embezzler at a large Midtown department store. I avoided telephoning Lily, lest I should seem nosy about her sleuthing progress. This restraint on my part meant, of course, that we did not see each other, which I found to be a strain, as we are used to spending frequent nights on the town, whether at dinner, a sports event, dancing, the opera, or a Broadway play.

Then one morning while I was at my desk typing letters Wolfe had dictated the day before, the phone rang, and for reasons I can't explain, I knew it was Lily.

"Have you missed me?" she asked.

"That's pretty good as a conversation starter," I told her. "I could play coy, of course, but instead I will own up. Of course, I have missed you, and quite a bit."

"Aren't you going to ask what I've been up to all this time?"

"I figure that if you want me to know something, you will tell me."

"Archie! You're not miffed, are you?"

"Not in the least, my dear. I have just wanted to give you some space with this—"

"Investigation," she said, finishing my sentence. "And I do thank you for your forbearing. As ever, you are a gentleman."

"*Forbearing.* A very good word."

"I believe I used it correctly. Would Nero Wolfe approve?"

"I am sure he would. I've heard it from him on numerous occasions. Now . . . just what have you been up to?"

Lily laughed. "Ah, so you *are* curious after all."

"Do you blame me?"

Another laugh. "I'd like to talk to you about what I've learned. May I take you to dinner—and at Rusterman's?"

"How can I say no to an offer like that?"

"I was hoping you couldn't. Come by for me in a taxi at seven fifteen, and I will make a seven thirty reservation."

When I pulled up in front of her building in a cab, Lily came out of the lobby, her high heels clicking on the sidewalk. I climbed out of the taxi, held open the door, and bowed as she stepped in; then I went around and got in through the street-side door.

"Ah, what a fine gesture," she said as I settled next to her.

"I was not about to make you slide all the way across the seat," I told her. "Only a cad would do that. Cabbie, take us to Ruster-man's Restaurant, as fast as this old chariot of yours can go."

"Right you are, Govn'r," he answered with a lame attempt at a British accent.

Felix, owner Marko Vukcic's right-hand man at the restaurant, seated us in a corner well removed from other diners and smiled at Lily, asking, "Is this table to your liking, Miss Rowan?"

"It certainly is, Felix. Thank you so much for remembering our favorite spot." He presented menus and a wine list, promised that our waiter would be with us shortly, then executed a snappy about-face and left us.

Lily turned to me with a grin. "After we order some wine and decide on our entrées—and remember, this is on me—I will give you a report on my recent activities."

"As a sleuth?"

"Well . . . I guess you could call it sleuthing. I was able to reach every one of the men Maureen had gone out with who was listed in her calendar."

"Congratulations."

"Not so fast with any plaudits; I really learned very little," Lily said. "Most of them had little or no idea where she had gone, and none thought that she had behaved in any strange way the last time each was with her."

"What about the last guy she was seen with, according to her calendar—Lloyd Thorne, wasn't it?"

"Ah, your memory is as sharp as ever. I talked to him in his office, and he was the only one who said he sensed some unease in Maureen."

"What did he say about her?"

Lily paused as I chose a wine and the waiter retreated. "With that memory of yours, you will of course remember that they went to the opera *Tannhäuser*. Thorne said from the moment he picked her up in a cab that night, Maureen was very distracted, not at all like she had been on previous occasions."

"Any idea how many dates they'd had?"

Lily shook her head. "As I mentioned to you before, she has never talked a lot about her social life, at least not to me. But I got the impression from Thorne that theirs was not an overly serious relationship."

"What else did he say about that night?"

"That Maureen was not her usual, talkative self on the way to the opera, at the intermissions, or when they had drinks later. 'She seemed to be somewhere else,' Thorne told me," Lily added as she pulled some sheets of paper out of her purse and read from them. "'I can't explain it exactly, except to say it was almost like I wasn't even there,' Thorne said. 'She didn't ask me anything about myself, as she had on previous occasions, and she didn't seem to be the least bit interested in any topic I brought up. Now you tell me that none of her friends has heard from her for days.'"

"How did Thorne seem to you?"

"Concerned, definitely. We talked in a conference room at his law firm, and he acted genuinely surprised that she had dropped out of sight. 'I can't imagine where she has gone to,' he said. 'She always seemed so well grounded to me, so self-confident.' He really had no suggestions as to anyone else I might talk to about her whereabouts."

"It sounds like the other men you spoke to also weren't really helpful," I said.

"They weren't. Each one was agreeable to meet me. I talked to Jason Reed, the book publisher, and Eric Mason, the ad man, in their offices. Will Talmadge, whose company makes electric cables, met with me in his apartment at the Dakota; and Clay Dalton and I had coffee at a café in Greenwich Village near where he lives. Each of them, like Thorne, said he had no idea where Maureen might have gone.

"Also, they all professed genuine affection for her, especially Eric Mason, the one she sees more frequently than the others. He seemed to be the most concerned about her. If I were to guess, I'd now say that something serious might be cooking between them."

"Interesting. Anything else to add?"

Lily paused and shook her head as if in disbelief. "Talmadge told me he thought it would be a good idea—no, make that a *great* idea—if he and I were to go out together sometime soon. He even suggested I might stay for a while in his apartment and have lunch with him, served by his own chef."

"And then after lunch?"

"We did not get that far. I told him, politely, I believe, that my social calendar is well filled, and it is likely to remain so for the foreseeable future."

"How did he take that?"

"Actually, quite well. My suspicion is that Mr. Talmadge is used to making similar suggestions to other women."

"And getting the kind of responses he got from you?"

"I cannot be certain, of course, but given the man's suavity— if that's even a word—I suspect that he is not always stymied in his, shall we say, *approaches*."

"I can only say that I am glad he was stymied on this occasion."

"You say the sweetest things to a girl, you smooth talker."

"Lord knows, I try."

# CHAPTER 5

We dined that evening on Rusterman's superb *squabs à la muscovite* and did not further discuss Maureen Carr's situation, other than to wonder about her brother.

"It's worth trying to find him," I said as we tackled desserts of raspberries in sherry cream (Lily) and blueberry pie à la mode (me).

"I agree, but I have absolutely no idea where to start. Now that my own foray into the world of detecting has proven to be less than satisfactory, I'm willing to let you have a go at the shadowy Everett Carr."

"You gave it a good try, my dear, and sometimes the things you don't learn can be as valuable is the ones you do. Can you recall anything Maureen ever said that might be of help regarding her brother?"

"I can't at the moment, but I will ask the other women

in our group, although I'm not optimistic about getting any results."

"Give it a try, tomorrow if possible, and get back to me."

Lily wasted no time the next day, although she called me in frustration at 9:00 a.m., as I was in the office opening the just-delivered mail.

"The good news is that I have reached all seven of what I refer to as our inner circle, not counting Maureen, of course. The bad news is that not a single one of them has any idea where Everett Carr lives—or anything else of substance about him, for that matter. The only shred of information is that Ellen Preston recalled Maureen telling her some months ago that she had happened to see her brother at a distance walking along Fifth Avenue, and that he looked like a vagrant. She went out of her way to avoid running into him."

"So at least we know he is probably in the city, for whatever that's worth. Consider me to be on the case."

"I have a feeling that I know where you're going next," Lily said. "Does the name Cohen have anything to do with it?"

The woman knows me too well. I picked up the telephone and dialed one of the numbers I know by heart. "Cohen! I'm on deadline!" the voice at the other end barked.

"You don't have to shout into the phone," I responded. "My hearing is just fine, thank you."

"All right, Archie," Lon Cohen snapped, his voice lowering several decibels. "What is it you need this time?"

"That's a fine way to respond to a call, especially a call from someone who helped fatten your wallet at poker last Thursday night."

"I can't help it, Archie, if you insist on raising with two pairs when it should have been obvious that I clearly had three of a kind."

"Hope springs eternal. Now, are you really on deadline, or is that just a way to discourage bothersome callers?"

"Obviously, it didn't work with you. To what do I owe this intrusion, Shamus?"

"I'm looking for information."

"Of course, you are. What's in it for me?"

"A bit early to tell. I want to know what you might have in your reference room about a man named Everett Carr."

"Is this something Nero Wolfe's working on?"

"Not at the moment, but . . ."

"Playing cagey, eh?"

"Me, cagey? Never," I told Lon. "However, if we learn anything you have on Mr. Carr that might be helpful to us, it might also lead to something helpful to you and your esteemed publication."

A bit of background here on Lon Cohen, for those of you who are new to these narratives. He toils for the *New York Gazette* and does not have a title I'm aware of, but his office on the twentieth floor of the *Gazette* building is just down the hall from the publisher, and Lon plays a major role in deciding what stories end up on page one of the fourth-largest newspaper in America. Over the years, he has been a great help to Nero Wolfe and me with information, but we have returned the favor by throwing at least a score of scoops to Lon and the *Gazette*.

"Okay, I will play along with you—for a while, at least," Lon said. "I'll have the boys downstairs pull the clips on this guy Carr, assuming we have any, and you can drop by and look at them. But remember who your friends are if it turns out there's a story here."

"I never forget who my friends are," I said, hanging up before he could mount a retort.

\* \* \*

A half hour later, I hoofed it north to the *Gazette*'s offices near the Chrysler Building, going straight to the reference room, or the "morgue" in newspaper terminology, which adjoins the city room, the paper's nerve center. "Hi, Mr. Goodwin, I have been expecting you. Haven't seen you in quite a while."

"It has been a long time, Bernie. Lon Cohen must have told you I was coming."

"That he did, Mr. G., and I've got the file that he told me you wanted to look at. 'Fraid there isn't a whole lot in it, though," he said, handing me a small manila envelope and steering me to a small desk. The *Gazette* does not allow its clippings to leave the building, no exceptions.

The Everett Carr file was indeed thin, with only two entries, each of them between three and five years old.

HANDBOOK RAIDED IN HELL'S KITCHEN

Police closed down a handbook on Eleventh Avenue at 54th Street last night. The
operator, Charles Spencer, 59, of 217 W.
83rd St., was booked on a charge of running
an illegal gaming facility.
The only other person on the premises at
the time was Everett Carr, who gave his age
as 44 and was released.

PEDESTRIAN STRUCK BY CAB IN TIMES SQUARE

Edna Frederickson, 49, of 229 E. 77th St.,
was struck by a Yellow cab at 43rd St. and
Seventh Ave. yesterday afternoon and taken
by ambulance to Bellevue Hospital, where

her injuries were described as minor.
A witness, Everett Carr, who declined to
supply his address, said Mrs. Frederickson
crossed 43rd St. when the "walk" sign was
lighted, and that the taxi struck her in the
crosswalk. The cabbie, Ed Watts, was cited
for reckless driving.

So much for learning about Everett Carr from the *Gazette*'s
clips, but I was ready with a Plan B. "Bernie, do you mind if I
page through your telephone directories?"

"Hey, I know what a good friend you are to Mr. Cohen, so,
sure, be my guest."

The *Gazette*, probably like most other daily papers, keeps a
batch of phone directories for the communities in its circulation
area and beyond. Bernie led me to the shelves where theirs are
stored.

We keep Manhattan and Brooklyn directories at the
brownstone, but as long as I was here . . . I tackled the fat
Manhattan book first, and you may or may not be interested
to learn that there are 157 Carrs listed, none of whom was
an Everett or simply an E. Carr. On to Brooklyn, also a lot
of Carrs, but no luck. Ditto with Queens, the Bronx, Staten
Island, Yonkers, the New Jersey cities just across the Hudson,
and the counties of Westchester and Nassau. I mention this as
a response to all those who have said to me, "Being a detective
must be so exciting."

I left the *Gazette* and went back to the brownstone, where we
would be having spareribs in Fritz's special sauce for lunch.
When I got home, it was still fifteen minutes before Wolfe's
descent from the plant rooms, so I called Lily and filled her in.

"No luck on trying to locate Everett Carr, although the sparse information on him in the *Gazette*'s files, along with Maureen's sighting of him on Fifth Avenue a while back, tends to suggest that he lives somewhere in this town and has been in a bookie joint."

"I will telephone Sofia, on the off chance she might know something about him," Lily said. "The subject did not come up when we were with her."

"It's better than anything that I can think of at the moment. You know where to reach me."

After a lunch at which Wolfe expounded on the reasons third-party candidates are unable to win presidential elections, I went for a walk to stretch my legs. As I passed a drugstore on Ninth Avenue, I had an inspiration, if you could so term it. I went inside, stepped into a pay telephone booth with my nickel, and dialed the number of the aforementioned Saul Panzer, the best freelance operative in North America and maybe beyond.

"Hi, Archie," he said. "The only time I've seen you lately is at our weekly poker games. Things slow these days for you and Nero Wolfe?"

"We haven't had much business lately, but we frankly haven't needed it after all the cases last month."

"Yeah, that was one busy time for you, me, Fred, and Orrie. And, of course, Wolfe." Saul was speaking about Fred Durkin and Orrie Cather, who with Saul are the freelance detectives Wolfe most often uses.

"I've got a question for you, one that won't bring you any money."

"Fire away," Saul said. "I'm not always mercenary, especially with a friend."

"Here's the situation: I'm working on something for Lily Rowan, and we're trying to find someone who may not want to be found."

"Happens a lot. Tell me about this individual."

"He's in his mid-to-late forties, probably single, and said to be careless with money."

"Alcoholic?"

"We're not sure."

"Would you call him poverty-stricken?" Saul asked.

"I really don't think so, no."

"That would tend to rule out flophouses. Off the top, I would suggest looking into that big YMCA on Thirty-Fourth near Ninth Avenue. It's said to be the largest Y in the country. You probably know the building I'm talking about; it must be about fifteen stories high."

"Yeah, I've been by it, but never inside. What kind of men live there?"

"All sorts, Archie. I've had occasion to go in a few times on investigations. Oh sure, there are some down-and-outers of various sorts, but it's quite a mix: young guys just starting out on jobs in the big city; retirees on a slim pension; visitors looking for a fairly cheap room; ex-husbands who're paying plenty in alimony and child support. The rooms are plain but clean, and it can be a good place for someone who wants to lose himself. Is that the situation with the person you're looking for?"

"It very well could be," I said. "Can someone stay there for a long time?"

"Yeah, I suppose so. On the other hand, some joes use it as a hotel. I know of one traveling salesman in kitchen goods on a tight budget who stays there every time he comes to town."

"Thanks, Saul. Maybe I'll pop into the Y and see what I can learn."

"A word of caution: the place is very protective of its guests. For instance, the cops have been known to drop in looking for people, sometimes just casting around for any perps they might find. The management doesn't like random sweeps, so whoever is manning the front desk may not answer any questions of yours."

"Knowing that, I will proceed accordingly."

# CHAPTER 6

Saul Panzer had described the YMCA well. In the hundreds of times I had passed it, I never paid much attention, but this was one big, impressive structure, especially for a place that was essentially a poor man's hotel—although by no means, as Saul had stressed, a flophouse.

That afternoon, after Wolfe had gone up to the plant rooms to play with his "concubines," as he refers to the orchids, I took a short walk to the Thirty-Fourth Street entrance of the Y. It was fronted by a green canopy, which lent a further degree of dignity to the building.

I stood near the door and stopped a sixtyish and slightly stooped man as he came out. "Pardon me, sir, but I'm looking for someone who—"

"I got no time, no time at all," he cut me off, walking east.

Next, I approached a stocky chap of about forty who wore a

battered fedora and a windbreaker and was about to enter the building. "Pardon me, sir, but I have a question."

"Yeah?" He looked me up and down and shrugged. "Well-dressed guy like you panhandling? Well, I haven't got a red cent on me, so just forget it."

"That's not my question, sir. I wonder if you know an Everett Carr who might live here?"

He shrugged again and frowned. "You know him?"

"No, but a friend told me to look him up when I came to town. Said he might be able to show me around."

"You sure that he lives here?"

"My friend thought so, but he wasn't positive."

"Well . . . there is an Everett down the hall from me, but I've never known his last name. That might be him. Everett's not a very common moniker, you know."

"Maybe you can introduce us," I said.

"Not likely, Mac. I heard at lunch earlier this week that he hasn't been seen for days. The guy who said that lives next door to him. He was damned puzzled and told me that Everett never said anything about going away."

"What kind of fellow is Everett?"

"Sounds to me like you don't know a lot about him."

"I really don't."

"Well, he's . . . unusual, I guess you would say. I really can't say I know Everett all that well, but—"

"Say, how about I buy you a cup of coffee or a beer—your choice?"

His square face broke into a grin. "I wouldn't say no to a glass of beer."

"Is there a good saloon nearby?" I asked, playing dumb as would befit a visitor to the city.

"Just around the corner on Ninth Avenue," he said, and

in less time that it takes to hail a taxi at Grand Central, we were on stools in Gabby's, a watering hole I had passed many times.

"I'm Alf," my new friend said, pumping my hand vigorously as the bartender placed two frosty glasses of Rheingold in front of us. "I'm really Alfred, a name I've never liked, but after that poor sap Alf Landon got steamrolled by FDR in the election some years back, I got tagged with the name by my Democratic friends, who thought that I had voted for Landon. I hadn't."

"I'm Archie," I replied, trying to look like I was enjoying the beer, which has never been my drink of choice.

"Where you from, Archie?" Alf asked.

"Small town in Ohio," I said, which technically was not a lie, if you go back a bunch of years. "Tell me about Everett Carr."

"Oh yeah, I almost forgot. As I said before, I really didn't know him well. He was a hard guy to get close to."

"How so?"

Alf screwed up his face. "Often, several of us would gather downstairs in the coffee shop and shoot the breeze, you know? A lot of the bunch I hang around with at the Y have led, well . . . somewhat bumpy lives, and we talked about our experiences. Good for the soul, they say. Anyway, Everett never, not even once, has said anything about his past, or anything else to do with him. Whenever somebody asked him a question about himself, he changed the subject. I can't tell if it's shyness, or what. Didn't your friend say anything to you about Everett?"

"No, just that I should look him up. He wasn't even positive Everett Carr lived at the Y, so maybe he really is a man of mystery."

"He sure is as far as I'm concerned. The only thing I can tell you about him is that he must like to play the ponies, because more than once I've seen him carrying the *Daily Racing Form*."

"Maybe the reason he doesn't say much around your bunch is that he's embarrassed about his gambling."

"Hah!" Alf said, dismissing my idea with the wave of a hand. "Archie, compared to some of the things we have told one another about our lives and what we've done, gambling on the horses is kid stuff."

"Do you know anything else about him, anything at all?"

"Not really," Alf said as he drank beer and licked his lips. "Except that one time at our lunch counter, he was paying the cashier for his sandwich and I was right behind him getting ready to pay myself. I happened to notice that when he opened his wallet, it looked like he had a stack of double sawbucks in there."

"Maybe he'd had a good day at the track, or with a bookie," I ventured.

"Yeah, I suppose," Alf said. "You don't often see that kind of dough in the Y. Hey!" he said, looking up at the clock behind the bar. "The time sort of got away from me. I've got me a stint at one of the Broadway theaters as an usher. Puts some walking-around money in my pocket, you know? I got to get up to my room and change into a white shirt and tie so I look good to the swells who're spending all that big money on their seats down near the stage. 'Course, I get to see the show, too, from in the back. After a few nights, though, it gets pretty boring."

"Well, I appreciate your time, Alf," I said.

"Hey, it's me who should be doing the appreciating," he said. "Thanks again for the beer, Archie. And I'm sure sorry I couldn't tell you more about Everett. Nobody can figure out where he could have gone."

"Maybe he hit it really big at the races and decided to move to a place up on Park Avenue."

Alf laughed. "Somehow, I doubt it. Them racetracks, they got the odds stacked against you. Say, if I run into Everett, I'll tell him you came by to see him. Is there some place I can get hold of you?"

"No, because I'll be going back home to Ohio tomorrow. Thanks anyway, Alf."

# CHAPTER 7

The next morning after Wolfe had gone up to the plant rooms, I called Lily. "Did you find out anything about Maureen's brother from Sofia?" I asked.

"I was just about to call you, and I am sorry to say that the maid seemed to know nothing about Everett, other than Maureen having once mentioned him having a birthday. Sofia said she had never seen the man, and she didn't think he and Maureen were at all close."

"I didn't fare much better than you," I told her, proceeding to describe my trip to the YMCA and my meeting with Alf.

"Well, at least you learned *something* about him," Lily said. "He's very withdrawn, or at least private, he plays the horses, and he has been seen carrying around a wad of money. The part about gambling on the horses isn't a total surprise, given that *Gazette* clipping you told me about."

"You have given me an idea."

"Care to share it?"

"Not just yet, but I assure you I will if things develop the way I hope they do."

"Ah, ever the man of mystery."

"No, not mystery, just bafflement. I may end up jousting with windmills, but anything is better than just sitting on my hands."

When Wolfe came down from the roof and rang for beer, I turned to face him. "I have a problem," I said.

"Go on."

I proceeded to describe my day's activities and concluded by saying, "I want to hire Saul, Fred, and Orrie to canvass all the bookie joints in town. And I will pay them out of my own funds."

"You will not!" Wolfe barked as he opened the first of two bottles of Remmers that Fritz had brought in. "I salute your desire to learn the whereabouts of Miss Rowan's friend and that of her brother, with the two occurrences likely connected. Unless you or Miss Rowan voices an objection, I propose we join forces on this gest."

"If gest means what I think it does, I believe Miss Rowan will find the idea interesting."

"First, you are free to look up the definition of the word in any of the dictionaries on our shelves. Second, we should not proceed until you discuss my proposal with Miss Rowan."

Wolfe had thrown me for a loop. I know he is somewhat fond of Lily, an exception to his usual attitude regarding women. But I hadn't expected him to suggest his taking an active role in the search for Maureen and Everett Carr.

"One, I'll take your word regarding the definition of gest. Two, I will telephone Lily, and I can guarantee that she will want to pay you."

"Please call her now."

I dialed a number I knew well, and Lily answered on the first ring. "Mr. Wolfe would like to speak to you," I said, nodding to Wolfe, who picked up his instrument while I stayed on the line.

"Miss Rowan, this is Nero Wolfe. Archie has kept me apprised of developments in your search for Maureen Carr and her brother, including your conversations with her consorts. I offer my services in this endeavor, and I may be of some assistance."

"I am delighted to hear that, Mr. Wolfe, and I will of course reimburse you for your time and effort."

"Reimbursement is not necessary, Miss Rowan. I have no cases at present, and my financial condition is secure. In fact, additional income at this time would place me in a different tax bracket, and I would be penalized by the Internal Revenue Service for earning more, irrational as that may sound."

Not only was that irrational, it was incorrect, but I was not about to contradict my boss. He wanted to help Lily, and I was damned if I was going to get in his way.

"All right, Mr. Wolfe," Lily said. "I am going to accept your very kind offer. How should we proceed?"

"Archie will fill you in on our plans."

After Wolfe hung up, abrupt as usual, I told Lily the program. "And you really want me to be present?" she said, surprised.

"Definitely. After all, you are the client. We will meet tonight at nine, assuming everyone can be present. I hope you are available at such late notice."

"I will make myself available," Lily said.

I made three calls and was fortunate, catching everyone at home. I was even more fortunate to learn they all could make it to the brownstone tonight, although I did not fill them in on the reason for the meeting.

When I told Wolfe, he suggested we invite Lily for dinner. I thought about telling him that he was becoming a softy but stifled the impulse. Things were moving along, so why mess with this small step in a positive direction?

Lily had eaten with us on a number of occasions, so she was comfortable in the dining room as we consumed Fritz's braised wild turkey, followed by apples baked in white wine, while Wolfe expounded on the railroads' vital role in the settling of the American West. After dinner, the three of us repaired to the office, Lily in the red leather chair at the end of Wolfe's desk as befits a client. Wolfe drank beer, while Lily and I had glasses of after-dinner wine.

Saul Panzer arrived first, at eight fifty, and if he was surprised at seeing Lily, he did not let it show. With his 140-pound frame, rumpled suit, flat cap, and semishaved mug that is two-thirds nose, Saul hardly looks like the best freelance operative I have ever known. But that he is.

"Miss Rowan, so good to see you," he said with the slightest of bows as he slid into one of the trio of yellow chairs lined up facing Wolfe's desk.

Fritz was manning the front door, and next to be ushered into the office was Fred Durkin, thick in the middle, thin on the top of the head, and second only to Saul in his ability to hold a tail. Fred might on occasion seem a little dense, but do not let that fool you. He is as tough as one of the Giants' defensive linemen and as brave and loyal as a bulldog. When he saw Lily, Fred blinked his surprise and mumbled a greeting, then sat next to Saul.

Last to arrive was Orrie Cather, suave, handsome, and aware of it. He's a good operative, but not as good as he thinks, and he always has believed that he would be better at my job than I am.

As long as I'm upright and aboveground, he will never have that opportunity.

Like Fred, Orrie was surprised at Lily's presence, but he recovered his aplomb and threw her a smile that he thinks women find irresistible. She gave him a nod and a slim smile in return.

"Gentlemen, thank you for coming tonight," Wolfe said. "Would any of you like to join us in a drink?"

Saul and Orrie opted for scotch and Fred asked for a beer, because that's what he always feels he should have when in Wolfe's presence. I filled the orders, and once everyone had settled in with their libations, Wolfe began. "I know you all have met Miss Rowan before, but you may be surprised at her presence tonight. I explain by stating that she is my client." Looks of wonder followed from Fred and Orrie.

"Here is the situation," Wolfe continued as he laid out the scenario of Maureen Carr and Everett both having vanished. "I believe the disappearance of the siblings is by no means a coincidence. Archie and Miss Rowan have searched Miss Carr's residence and have found no substantive clues as to her possible whereabouts. And Archie has been unable to locate Everett Carr, although he has learned of Mr. Carr's predilection for betting on racehorses, particularly using handbooks, or 'bookies,' as they are called in the patois of the street and in the press. Archie?" he turned to me.

"Everett Carr was in a bookie joint at Eleventh Avenue and Fifty-Fourth Street that got raided several years ago, although he was not charged," I said, consulting my notes. "The place probably isn't operating anymore. At the time, the bookmaker, Charles Spencer, who did get cited, was living at 217 West Eighty-Third. I was able to find almost nothing else about Carr in a search of the *Gazette*'s files."

"I'm on the case, as far as this Spencer is concerned," Saul said.

Orrie Cather jumped in. "Hey, I can go after that one and—"

"Go ahead, Saul," Wolfe interrupted. "Orrie and Fred, there will be enough assignments for both of you. I have no idea how many bookmakers operate in New York, but I can imagine the numbers run at least into the dozens."

"That is true," Saul affirmed. "They show up in all sorts of places—barbers, cigar stores, magazine and newspaper shops, shoeshine parlors, small grocers. I even know of one handbook across the river in Long Island City that was run out of a tattoo joint."

"I suggest Mr. Panzer divide up the city and assign areas to Fred and Orrie—and to himself, as well. I realize this may be a fool's errand, but we must start somewhere," Wolfe said. "And there is a chance that one among this multitude of bookmakers may know the whereabouts of Mr. Carr. I remain convinced that locating him may well be the channel through which we will locate his sister."

"What about me? I can canvass some of those bookies, as well," I said.

"For the present, you and Miss Rowan should concentrate on finding Maureen Carr. However, I also suggest you act as a clearinghouse for reports from Saul, Fred, and Orrie," Wolfe said, turning to Lily.

"Miss Rowan, do you have anything to add to what has been discussed?"

"No, I believe you have covered everything that I can think of. And with Archie's help, I will continue trying to find people who have had some connection to Maureen, however tenuous."

Wolfe levered himself upright. "I again thank each of you for your time and wish you a good evening," he said, striding out of the office. His abrupt exit was no surprise to anyone in the room, as each of us is used to his curt behavior.

"All right, to echo Lily, I think the situation has been well laid out. Does anybody have questions?" I asked

"Yeah, I do," Orrie said as he walked over to the bar table against the wall and poured himself a second scotch. "What reason are we supposed to give these bookies for asking about Everett Carr?"

"Use your imagination," Saul snapped. "You can tell them Carr owes you dough and you want to find him. That seems like a reasonable excuse. Or you can say you gave him money to place on a nag that won at Belmont or wherever, and he's never showed up to pay you."

"I like both of those approaches," Fred put in. "Me, I plan to say that Carr is a cousin, and I want to find him so that I can pay off the loan he gave me."

"That sounds phony to me, Durkin," Orrie said. "Who would ever go asking a stranger to help finding someone so *you* could pay *them*? That doesn't make any sense."

I joined in. "Orrie, like Saul said, use your imagination. As long as the bookie doesn't think you're trying to horn in on his territory or that you are a plainclothes cop looking to run him in, he has no reason to be suspicious of you.

"You have told me before how you are able to charm even the most resistant women. Well, why don't you use some of that legendary charm on the bookies?"

That drew laughs all around, including from Lily. Orrie blushed and grinned, but it was easy for all of us to see that his self-professed success with the ladies was being recognized, and he liked the attention.

"Okay, now let us get serious," Saul said. "Because for some period of time Everett Carr had lived at that big YMCA on

Thirty-Fourth Street, it makes sense to start looking for bookies in that area, which I will undertake myself. And I will also see if that Spencer bookie who got nailed still lives up on Eighty-Third Street.

"Orrie, you take the rest of Manhattan, which I know is one big chunk of real estate, but with your connections, I'm sure you can ferret out a lot of bookmaking establishments. Somebody at one or more of them may know Carr."

"I'll start first thing tomorrow," Orrie said. "What about talking to people at the tracks, like touts and other old-timers who hang on the rails and seem to know everything about the horses and jockeys and stuff like drugging?"

"Unfortunately, none of the local tracks—Belmont, Aqueduct, or Jamaica—is open for the season yet, and they won't be until a few weeks from now when it gets warmer," Saul said, "so all we've got at present is the bookies. Fred, you have always known Brooklyn well, why don't you tackle that noble borough? And that should be enough for now. If nothing turns up on our Mr. Carr in our travels, then we'll venture out to Queens and the Bronx, and maybe even beyond."

"So there is the plan," I said. "All of you check in with me at least once every day, and Lily and I will be chasing down leads of our own."

# CHAPTER 8

*Chasing* became the operative word for Lily and me, starting the next day. After breakfast, I went to her apartment and we sat in the morning room with coffee and tried to figure out who she might have overlooked among Maureen's friends and acquaintances.

"I know that you have talked to her closest friends, the ones both of you are in that group with," I told her. "And you also have met with the men she has been with most recently. Who does that leave?" I spread my hands, palms up.

Lily thought for several seconds before speaking. "Well, I probably should get in touch with the people who head the organizations Maureen has been most closely involved with."

"They are. . . ?"

"A women's and children's aid society, a home for unwed mothers, and an orphanage. I hate to see you and Mr. Wolfe spend so much time with this. I feel like I've pushed both of you into my problem."

"First, you never pushed me into this; I have jumped in with both feet, ready to help. And nobody ever pushes Nero Wolfe into anything he doesn't want to do, either literally or figuratively. Now about the people who run these groups—I assume they are all women."

"They are, and I know each of them fairly well," Lily said. "I'm afraid I will have to tell them about Maureen's disappearance, and I really need to talk to them in person."

"No question whatever. Does that bother you?"

"Oh, a little, but I don't think we can keep the situation under wraps any longer. Besides, the men whom I talked to about Maureen already know something isn't right, and it's just a matter of time before they start calling me to ask what I've heard from or about her."

"Good point. Would you feel comfortable having me along when you talk to these fine women?"

"Oh, Archie, I really am leaning on you, and I'm sorry, but playing detective is certainly not my métier."

"No need to be sorry, and despite what you say, your instincts are good. I think you'd make a good shamus."

"I assume 'shamus' is some sort of a synonym for private eye."

"Some sort. I'm ready to accompany you to these meetings, assuming you are able to set them up."

"That should be no problem. I'll start calling now."

I went to the next room, which I would describe as a den, to give Lily privacy for her calls. Fifteen minutes later, I was reading the current copy of *Time* when she walked in and announced that she had set up appointments today for all three of these paragons of good works without telling them the reason for the meetings.

"Weren't they curious?"

"They were, but I merely told them it was a subject that I preferred not to discuss on the telephone."

"Now, of course, they are more curious than ever," I said, laughing. "Who are you talking to first?"

"Emily Ferris; she's the one who oversees the home for abandoned and orphaned children. She said she could see us there at any time today. I suggested eleven o'clock."

"Which means we need to get going. Did you tell her that I would be with you?"

"I did, and she was fine with that. She remembers meeting you once."

"Then she has the better of me. Where's the orphanage?"

"On the Upper East Side, Eighty-Ninth Street."

A Yellow cab, driven by a dour hackie who muttered about the mayor's many faults, got us to our destination ten minutes early. The building, an unadorned four-story brick number with a currently unoccupied playground on one side, was separated by high metal fencing from the noisy FDR Drive, and just beyond it, the gray waters of the East River.

In the small entry hall, a white-haired receptionist behind a window with a sliding panel recognized Lily and gave her a dimpled grin. "Hello, Miss Rowan, it is so nice to see you again. Mrs. Ferris is expecting you; I will buzz her."

"Thank you so much, Doris. It is good to see you again, as well. I hope your husband has recovered from his back troubles."

"He has indeed, Miss Rowan; he's almost as good as new, and thank you for asking. Here's Mrs. Ferris."

Emily Ferris stepped into the entry hall and greeted Lily with a hug and a kiss on the cheek. She was small and full-figured, with auburn hair, bangs, and a sunny expression. "And a hello to you, Mr. Goodwin," she said. "You may remember that we met a few years ago at a benefit auction in the Commodore Hotel."

"I do remember, of course," I said, finally recognizing her from our very brief moment at that frenzied function. "To Lily's friends, I'm Archie, none of this 'Mr.' business."

"Archie it is," she said, patting my arm. "Let's go to my office."

Once we were settled, Emily Ferris behind her plain wooden desk and Lily and I facing her in equally plain wood chairs, our hostess said to Lily, "Well, my curiosity is piqued. I do hope this visit does not mean that we have misused any of the funds your group has so generously given to us."

"Oh no, not at all. I have heard no complaints whatever about the way the orphanage is being run, quite the contrary. The reason we are here is to talk about Maureen Carr."

"Funny that you should mention Maureen," Emily said. "I was just this morning wondering why I haven't heard from her for some time now. She usually calls or stops by at least once a week, sometimes more often."

"Nobody else we know has heard from her for some time, either," Lily replied. "She seems to have disappeared without leaving any clue as to where she might be. We were hoping you might know something about her whereabouts."

The orphanage director wore a shocked expression. "My heavens! Let me see, the last time I saw Maureen was"—she opened what turned out to be a datebook—"yes, here it is. We had lunch three weeks ago yesterday, and she seemed just fine, very cheerful."

"And Miss Carr didn't mention any trips she was planning?" I asked.

"No, not at all. I'm trying to recall what she said about her-self that day. I don't think she mentioned anything particular she was doing. But that is like Maureen. She doesn't talk a lot about herself. She always seems more interested in what others are up to."

"That is typical of her, all right," Lily said. "When you were with Maureen at lunch, did she seem to be worried or distracted in any way?"

"Not at all, as I said. I'm still trying to think of anything she might have told me that would indicate some sort of problem, but I am sorry, nothing occurs to me.

"Oh, wait—Maureen had asked about my family and what we were doing, and I filled her in on our activities, which were nothing special. I thought I should respond with a question about her own family, which as far as I know consists of just the one brother, so I felt I should ask how he was.

"Her upbeat mood suddenly got dark, and just for a moment I saw . . . I don't know quite how to put it . . . I opened a door into a part of her life that I probably should not have. Then, like in the blink of an eye, she was her old self again. But I wish I hadn't been so nosy."

"You weren't nosy, you were just being friendly and support-ive," Lily assured her.

"I suppose so," Emily said, "but now, given what you've told me, I have to wonder if her disappearance is somehow tied in with her brother . . . Everett is his name, right?"

"Yes. Had she ever talked to you about him before?" I asked.

"Only in passing, and never with any details. I couldn't even tell you what he does for a living, or where he lives, although I'm sure their parents must have left both him and Maureen com-fortable financially. After all, I do know a little about Maureen's past."

"If you hear anything from her, please let me know," Lily said as we rose to leave.

"I ask the same of you," Emily Ferris responded. "I simply can't imagine where she could have gone."

I won't bore you with the descriptions of our conversations with the women who oversee the children's aid society and the unwed mothers' home, as neither of them had anything to add regarding Maureen's disappearing act.

"Have you got any other suggestions?" I asked Lily as we left the last of our meetings.

"Not at the moment, except to check back with the members of our group to see if any of them has news."

I dropped Lily off at home and returned to the brownstone. Wolfe was indulging in his afternoon session in the plant rooms, and I found a note on my desk from Fritz that read, "Call Mr. Panzer."

"Goodwin replying to your summons," I said into the mouthpiece when Saul picked up his phone.

"Archie, I got hold of that bookie, Spencer, although he's not a bookie anymore; he went straight—well, sort of. He now runs a pawnshop in Yorkville, which is where I talked to him. Anyway, that's neither here nor there. He remembered Everett Carr as a regular who came into his handbook damned near every day. 'That guy loved playing the ponies,' Spencer told me, 'but he didn't seem to know the first thing about handicapping. It got so that I almost felt sorry for the guy, because he ended up almost always backing losers.'"

"Did it seem to Spencer that Everett Carr had deep pockets?" I asked.

"I asked him that, of course, and he laughed. 'That's why I was *almost* sorry for him; it seemed like he was always carrying a thick wad, and I don't mean Abes, but double sawbucks and fifties and even the occasional C-note. And it didn't seem to bother him much when he came up a loser, which sadly happened most of the time.'"

"Does Spencer still see Carr?"

"Not at all," Saul replied. "He said that after he got busted, he got out of the bookie business altogether, and he cut his ties with all his old customers at his wife's insistence. The last time he saw Carr was the day the cops shut Spencer down and hauled him in."

"Pick anything else up from other bookies?"

"Not much at all. Oh, there is one named Leon. He operates out of a cigar store on Thirty-Second Street, and he told me there's somebody he knows only as 'Everett,' who he thought was living at the Y. He said Everett came in like clockwork until recently, and then just stopped."

"Was Carr just as unsuccessful at this establishment as with Spencer?"

"That's what I picked up. Our man gambled heavily and never got upset when he lost, according to Leon, who said, 'the guy seemed to have a bottomless pit of money, although he dressed more like a vagrant than a swell.'"

"That's the extent of what I've learned, Archie, which is not much. I can hit a few more places tomorrow. Heard anything from Fred or Orrie?"

"Not yet, but I expect they will be checking in. If you haven't got anything else on your plate right now, you could visit a few more bookies, but I'm not sure you're going to learn anything more about our elusive gambler."

No sooner had I hung up with Saul than Fred checked in. "I've been to more darned bookies than I ever knew existed in Flatbush and the far reaches of Brooklyn, and it seems that nobody running those joints knows one single thing about Everett Carr. That assumes, of course, that he uses his real name when he's laying down bets."

"He's been up front about his name on this side of the East River," I told Fred. "He does not appear to be ashamed of his gambling proclivities."

"'Proclivities,' that's a word Mr. Wolfe would use, right, Archie? I even know what it means."

I told Fred I was proud of him and said he should spend one more day with the bookies in Brooklyn and then report back. He didn't grumble because like most other freelance operatives, he was just glad to be working, even in the short term.

That left Orrie, and I didn't hear from him until just before Wolfe came down from playing with the posies at six. "Archie, I've been all over this island coming across all sorts of hand-books in all kinds of places. I have been smart enough never to get sucked in by horse racing, so I'm getting quite an education," he said from a phone booth.

"I am sure glad to learn that you're improving your knowledge of the city where you've spent your whole life. But more to the point, have you found anything out about Everett Carr and where he might be?"

"Well . . . no, but it hasn't been for lack of trying, Archie. I've walked my tail off, and I haven't met a single one of these guys who's ever heard of Everett Carr. Maybe he gives another name, probably a phony one, when he makes bets."

"Fred suggested the same thing, and I told him Carr has used both his first and last names when betting. Here's one thing you can do tomorrow: ask each bookie if there's been a gambler in his place who seems to have a lot of dough to throw around, as in wads of it. And one who is not very successful in his wagering."

Orrie grumbled about what he thought was a waste of time, but like Fred, he has never said no to Wolfe's money, so I did not have to twist his arm to keep him focused on the job.

Once Wolfe was settled behind his desk with his predinner beer, I gave him a report, and he grunted. "Does Miss Rowan know where Maureen Carr does her banking?" he asked.

"I don't know, but I can find out."

"Do so."

That's Wolfe for you. When giving orders, never use a lot of words when one or two will be adequate. I dialed Lily and posed the question to her.

"I'm almost positive it's the Continental Bank and Trust Company," she said, "although I'm not sure which branch Maureen uses." She didn't ask why I wanted to know, so I thanked her, ended the call, and turned to Wolfe with the answer.

"Satisfactory," he said, which for Wolfe is an effusive reply, especially given the seemingly mundane nature of the question and answer. But I was about to get an explanation for his enthusiasm.

"Get Mr. Hotchkiss on the telephone. I want to speak to him." Another tersely worded order.

A few words here about Mortimer M. Hotchkiss: He is a longtime vice president of the Continental Bank, where my boss has been a depositor for years—make that a depositor with a balance that averages close to six figures. Hotchkiss is always available to talk to Wolfe, and today was no exception. I got through to his secretary quickly, and she put the banker on the line while I stayed on as well.

"Ah, Mr. Wolfe, it is so good to hear from you," he said. "I do hope that nothing is amiss."

"It is not, sir, although I am in need of some information."

"Anything I can do to help you will be my pleasure," Hotch-kiss replied.

"You had better wait until you hear my request. I am in search of knowledge regarding another of your depositors, one who may very well be in a life-threatening situation."

After a pause on the other end, Hotchkiss cleared his throat before speaking. "I know, Mr. Wolfe, that you are aware of how highly we value privacy where our customers are concerned."

"I would expect nothing less of you in the way of rectitude, and I will be as discreet as possible. I am going to speak a name, and if you remain silent upon hearing it, I will assume that individual is among your customers. And if I ask other questions and you remain silent, I will take that silence as an assent."

"All right . . ." Hotchkiss replied in an uneasy tone, "although I may need time to call up some records."

"So be it," Wolfe said as he pronounced Maureen Carr's name. I could hear Hotchkiss muttering to someone, presumably his secretary, who gave him a whispered reply. Records likely were on their way to his office.

Wolfe waited almost two minutes by my watch and received no response from the banker.

"Did the individual whose name I uttered recently withdraw a large sum from your institution?" Again, no response.

"Did that sum equal or exceed fifty thousand dollars?"

Still the banker remained mum.

After another minute-plus had elapsed, Wolfe spoke. "Thank you very much for your time and your patience, Mr. Hotchkiss," Wolfe said.

"You are most welcome, Mr. Wolfe. As I have said many times in the past, Continental appreciates and values your business and the trust that you have placed in our institution. I look forward to many more years of our association."

"Spoken as only a banker can speak," I told Wolfe after we had hung up.

"Mr. Hotchkiss represents tradition and a strong sense of duty, which is not to be dismissed lightly at a time when tradition and dedication to duty are too frequently denigrated as being old-fashioned values."

"Well, I thought your figuring out that a big withdrawal was made and your way of dealing with that tradition and duty was damned cute. Hotchkiss can't be accused of violating a customer's trust. Also, wasn't it a nice coincidence that both you and Maureen Carr use the same bank? No wonder you said 'satisfactory' to me."

"Coincidence, perhaps," Wolfe said, flipping a palm. "But Continental is the biggest bank in the city, so to use one of your sports terms, I was playing the odds."

# CHAPTER 9

So now we knew almost surely that Maureen had withdrawn a healthy sum from her account at the Continental Bank & Trust Company. I say *almost surely* because we were relying on the words—or lack thereof—from Mortimer M. Hotchkiss. However, I knew Wolfe felt comfortable in the knowledge that Hotchkiss was playing straight with us. And knowing the banker almost as well as Wolfe does, I also felt he gave us the information we requested without having to utter a single word.

"You need to apprise Miss Rowan of this development," Wolfe said as he picked up his current book, *Crusade in Europe*, by Dwight D. Eisenhower.

Lily may not be a fee-paying client, but to Wolfe, she is a client nonetheless, as he was reminding me. I called her and laid out what we had learned from the banker.

I was met with silence for several seconds, and when she spoke, it was in measured and somber tones.

"I do not like what I have heard. Does Mr. Wolfe have an explanation, or a conjecture?"

"Not so far. I'm sure we will be discussing the situation. What are your thoughts?"

"I . . . I don't know. Fifty thousand dollars, if that really is the figure; what a lot to withdraw at once. And for what reason?"

"It could take Maureen a lot of places, including around the world on an ocean liner," I said, trying to lighten the mood. I failed.

"Be serious! Something bad has happened to her, really bad, I am sure of it. I have thought so all along, and now this . . ."

"As I said, Mr. Wolfe and I are going to talk, and we will let you know what the next moves will be."

Lily clearly was not satisfied, and I did not blame her.

After we hung up, I swiveled toward to Wolfe. "Lily isn't happy with what's happened, as you no doubt could tell from my end of the conversation."

He set down his book and scowled. "What would you have me do?" he demanded.

"You are the genius in this operation. Figure something out."

"Pfui. I will not be badgered!"

"Way back in the dark ages, you hired me to be a burr under your saddle, among my other duties. So that's what I am being—a burr."

Wolfe's response was to pick up the book and continue reading. I had been dismissed, a not-unusual occurrence in the office.

When we reached an impasse like this one, I had several options: one, I could go for a walk; two, I could continue to badger Wolfe; or three, I could threaten to resign. As I was mulling these options, the phone jangled and I answered, as usual, "Nero Wolfe's office, Archie Goodwin speaking."

"Mr. Goodwin, this is Eric Mason. You may not recall this, but we met briefly at Lily Rowan's penthouse last year, where she was having a cocktail benefit for one of her charities."

"Yes, I do remember you, Mr. Mason. You're with the ad agency Gordon and Grove, and Lily has told me you have won a lot of creative awards."

"You have a good memory, and you are too kind. I know from Lily that you work for Nero Wolfe, and I would, uh . . . like to hire him."

"Really? May I ask for what purpose?"

"To find the woman I intend to marry—Maureen Carr."

That stopped me in my tracks. "What do you know about Miss Carr at present?"

"I am aware, of course, that she has disappeared. And you probably know that Lily came to see me recently to ask if I had any idea where she was."

"Yes, I do know that she talked to you. And you told her you couldn't imagine where she had gone."

"That is correct, and I have been unable to reach Maureen for more than two weeks now. Also, no one I have talked to who knows her has any clue as to where she is."

"You may be aware that Mr. Wolfe charges extremely high rates for his services."

"So I have heard, and I am confident that I can afford those rates."

"I do not doubt that, but I am unsure of Mr. Wolfe's willingness to take on your assignment."

"I would like to come to his office—I know he rarely leaves home—and talk to him face-to-face."

"I will have to confer with Mr. Wolfe. Please give me the best telephone number where I can reach you."

Mason gave me a number and asked, "When am I likely to hear from him—or you?"

"I can't say for sure, but I promise I will do my best to give you a response within a day or so."

He started to impress upon me the urgency of his request, and I said that everyone who wants to employ Nero Wolfe is in a hurry. I finally had to tell him I had other business and terminated the call.

"Well, I just got thrown a curveball," I told Wolfe, or whoever that was hiding behind the Eisenhower memoir.

He put the book down. "Another of your time-worn baseball aphorisms. Very well, report." He sighed.

I recounted verbatim my conversation with Eric Mason, which was hardly a challenge, given its brevity. "So here is a potential client, and a very prosperous one," I concluded.

"I already have a client!" he barked.

"You do only if you have decided you are going the pro bono route," I countered. "You often have told me how much money it takes to support this operation, and as I am the keeper of the checkbook and of our financial records, I am well aware of the cash flow necessary to keep this grand old building afloat."

"I am committed to Miss Rowan—you of all people should know that."

"And I am pleased that you are, for both professional and personal reasons. However, it appears that both she and Eric Mason have the same goal, the locating of Maureen Carr. I hardly think Lily would object if the two of them became 'joint clients,' with one paying the freight."

Wolfe leaned back, closed his eyes, and spread his arms out on the desk, palms down. "I know little about this man, other than what has been reported and described by both you and Miss Rowan."

"You have nothing whatever to lose by seeing him. If he doesn't measure up to your standards, then, okay, consider that he's out of the picture. And if he seems to you to be a decent sort, then you can ask Miss Rowan if she has any objection to his being a co-client."

Wolfe doesn't like it when I argue with him, but he knows I am his equal in stubbornness, if that's even a word. He said nothing for several beats, then drew in a bushel of air, exhaled, and said, "Very well. Communicate with Mr. Mason and tell him to be here at nine p.m. tonight."

I dialed the number he had given to me, and on the first ring, he crisply said, "Mason here."

"Archie Goodwin on this end. Nero Wolfe can see you at nine tonight." I gave him our address.

"I hoped that was you calling. Excellent. Is there anything I should be prepared for?"

"Just that you will have some questions tossed your way, probably quite a batch of them. How you answer will depend on whether you will become a client, not to put too much pressure on you."

Mason chuckled. "Hey, I'm in the ad business, Mr. Goodwin, which is nothing if not a pressure cooker. If I couldn't handle it, I would have been out on my tail a long time ago."

"See you at nine. Be prompt," I told him.

In the next half hour, Saul, Fred, and Orrie all checked in, and none of them reported having any success at all in learning more about Everett Carr from the bookies they had visited. I told each of them to cease any further work until they heard back from me.

\* \* \*

Eric Mason was more than prompt that evening. He rang our bell at eight fifty, and I swung open the front door to his grin. He must have come straight from work, because he was dressed like a model in a men's fashion magazine, and he wore his clothes well on his slender six-foot-plus frame. "You look sharp," I told him.

"Don't make too much of it," he replied. "Because I'm in the agency's creative department, I usually dress casually, but late this afternoon, we had to give a campaign presentation to a Newark bank, and their bunch always dresses in three-piece pinstripes and the like, so we figured we needed to dress like they do."

"Did it work?" I asked as we walked down the hall to the office.

"Too early to tell. They're still digesting what we showed them, but I am confident we will get the account."

Wolfe looked up as we entered the office, and I made the introductions, gesturing Mason to the red leather chair.

"Would you like something to drink, sir? As you can see, I am having beer."

"I'll have a scotch and water, thanks," our guest said, crossing one leg over the other. I went to the wheeled cart and played bartender, handing Mason his drink and settling in at my desk with my notebook.

"Now, Mr. Mason, I understand you wish to hire me to search for Maureen Carr, is that correct?"

"It is," he said after taking a sip of his drink and nodding approvingly. I had poured from our best label.

"Do you have any idea about her whereabouts, or why she disappeared?"

"I do not, Mr. Wolfe, and I am at a total loss to understand what has happened to her. The last time we were together, which was . . . well, almost three weeks ago now, I had asked Maureen to marry me."

"And the woman's response?" Wolfe asked.

Mason took a deep breath. "Maureen told me she had been expecting my proposal for some time, so she already had given it some thought—a lot of thought, she said. And she told me she was flattered but wanted time to think it over."

"Your reaction?"

"I had mixed feelings. I was not surprised that she saw my proposal coming, but of course I was hoping for a more definite—that is to say positive—response."

Wolfe drank beer and set his stein down. "It is my understanding you were by no means the only man spending time with Miss Carr."

"That is correct," Mason said, running a hand over sandy hair that showed signs of going gray. "Maureen is a social animal, and I mean that only in a positive sense. She enjoys going out on the town, and she has had numerous escorts, all of whom I know. But those relationships are not what I would call in any sense serious. These men are confirmed bachelors, while I would like to get married again, and the woman I plan to marry, if she will have me, is Maureen Carr."

"You think you know this woman well enough to propose marriage, yet you have no idea where she is or why she has 'vamoosed,' to use a term of Mr. Goodwin's," Wolfe said.

"Vamoose makes it sound as if Maureen chose to leave," Mason said, "but I have to feel that her disappearance was not voluntary."

"Do you have a theory about that?"

Mason appeared flustered. "I really don't. As I said before, I am at a total loss as to where she might be—and why."

Wolfe was being patient. "What do you know about Miss Carr's past, her family, her upbringing? If she is indeed your intended, you must be curious about her history."

"I know Maureen's parents are dead, and that her father was an executive—the principal owner, really—of a steel company somewhere in the Pittsburgh area. I also know that she graduated from Radcliffe with a major in English, and that she worked for a time as a proofreader and then as an editor at a publishing house, Ferris and Reed. When she was there, she met my friend Jason Reed, and he introduced us."

"Hasn't Mr. Reed been among her escorts?"

"Yes, that's true, but their relationship is not romantic, as he has gone out of his way to tell me. Jason has been seen around town with more different dates than I can keep track of. He likes to be seen with pretty women, but he seems to have no interest whatever in a serious relationship. In fact, he has encouraged my involvement with Maureen."

Wolfe made a face. He doesn't like hearing about romantic affairs, so I stepped in. "Does Miss Carr have any siblings?" I asked.

"Yes . . . one, a brother, Everett. Actually, he is a half brother, as they had different mothers."

"How would you describe their relationship?"

Mason furrowed his brow, as if lost in thought. "They really aren't at all close, and she almost never mentions him."

"Is there any reason for that?" I asked.

More brow furrowing. "Well . . . Everett, whom I never have met, seems to be something of a black sheep in the family. He of course inherited a substantial amount, as did Maureen, but he apparently has chosen to lead an . . . well, an unconventional lifestyle."

"In what way?"

"Based on what I have gathered from Maureen, he has never held a job, nor does he have any interest at all in working."

"One of the advantages of being born with a silver spoon in your mouth," I observed.

"I suppose so. What success I've had has been earned, not inherited. Everett doesn't seem to care about where he lives or how he dresses, according to Maureen. When I asked what occupies his time, she said his major interest is betting on racehorses."

"You have given us very little to go on, sir," Wolfe said. "Might Miss Carr have decamped with her brother?"

"I hardly think so. As I said, she never talks about Everett, and on the few times I've brought him up in conversation, she ignores my question or she just changes the subject."

Wolfe sighed. "You need to know that there already is an individual who has requested that I attempt to locate Miss Carr."

"Well, why in the hell didn't you or Goodwin tell me that when I called? It appears that I've come here for nothing!" Mason barked, rising.

Wolfe held up a palm. "Please sit down, Mr. Mason. I have no reason why you and this person cannot both engage me."

"Based on what I've heard, I would have expected better of you, Mr. Wolfe," Mason said, still in a state. "Charging two people for the same job!"

"Wait, please," Wolfe replied in an even tone. "The other individual involved is not paying me, for reasons that may become evident later."

"Just who is this?"

"Until I learn if my existing client is comfortable with you joining forces, I cannot reveal a name."

"Well, that is one hell of a pickle," Mason said, holding up his empty glass. Ever alert, I got him a refill.

"Let me propose this," Wolfe said. "We will communicate with this person and find out how to best proceed."

"When do you plan to do that?" Mason was flushed with anger.

"Right now," Wolfe said, looking at me. I got the not-so-subtle hint and dialed Lily's number. When she answered, I said, without preamble, "I am sitting in the office with Nero Wolfe and a gentleman named Eric Mason. Mr. Wolfe would like to speak to you." I turned to Wolfe, who picked up his instrument.

"Here is the situation," he said, "Mr. Mason has proposed to engage me to find Maureen Carr. I have explained to him that I already am committed to an individual who also seeks to ascertain the whereabouts of Miss Carr."

"Are you avoiding speaking my name?" Lily asked from her end of the line.

"I am."

"All right, I get it. I have no objection whatever to Mason becoming your client. I will drop out."

"I am not suggesting that, not for a moment."

"So you will take both of us on?"

"That is my intent."

"All right, what comes next?" Lily asked.

"Do you have any objection to speaking to Mr. Mason—right now?"

"No, not at all. I assume he does not know who you have on the line."

"That is correct. Mr. Mason, will you please pick up Mr. Goodwin's telephone?"

Mason shrugged and leaned over to take the phone. "Hello, who is this?" he said.

"Hello, Eric. You know me."

"That voice—I know it. Is it . . . can it be . . . Lily Rowan?"

"It can indeed," she replied. "Welcome aboard. That is, if you have no objection to partnering with me."

"Uh, no, no objection of any kind," he said, taken aback by this development. "I know you have been a good friend of

Maureen's for a long time, far longer than I've known her, so I should not be surprised at your concern for her."

"We both seem to have the same goal," Lily said.

"I totally agree." Mason turned to Wolfe. "What is the next step?"

"I suggest you both meet here with me and Mr. Goodwin. Are you both available tomorrow night, at nine o'clock?"

"I will make myself available," Mason said.

"So will I," Lily seconded, "although it will mean breaking a date with Archie to go dancing at the Churchill. I am confident he will take this setback in stride."

"I am licking my wounds, but somehow they will heal," I said, loud enough so that Lily could hear through the telephones that Wolfe and Mason were holding close to me.

"That's a good lad, I am so proud of you," she retorted in a strong tone that carried easily to me.

"If this raillery has reached its conclusion, I have other business to attend to," Wolfe said, rising and leaving the office. That "other business" almost surely would be a discussion with Fritz about tomorrow's lunch and dinner.

# CHAPTER 10

The next night, Eric Mason arrived at the brownstone at eight thirty-five. "You are even earlier than before," I told him as I swung open the front door and he entered.

"That is by design," he responded as I took his coat and hung it up. "I would like to speak to you and Mr. Wolfe without Lily Rowan being present."

I didn't question his reason as I walked him down the hall. Wolfe looked up from his book when we entered the office and then glanced at the clock on the wall with a questioning expression.

"I know that I am early, Mr. Wolfe," Mason said as I steered him to one of the yellow chairs. "The reason is that I want you to know I'm perfectly comfortable with Lily Rowan not paying any of the fee for your search for Maureen. I realize both of you have a special relationship with Lily, and I know her well enough to recognize that she is an individual of sterling character. I am happy to be partnering with her."

"We are in agreement in our appraisal of Miss Rowan," Wolfe said, drinking beer and showing no irritation at having been interrupted in his reading. "She has been a welcome visitor in this house for many years. Would you like something to drink?"

Mason grinned and nodded as I asked, "The usual?"

Just as our guest was settled with a scotch, the doorbell rang again, and I went to admit Lily. "Mr. Mason already is here," I told her, "but I have reserved the red leather chair for you as befits your station."

"How very gallant," she said as I took her coat and we went to the office. As Lily clicked in, garbed in stylish pumps and a robin's-egg blue dress, Mason snapped to his feet like an enlisted man at the arrival of a full-bird colonel. Wolfe remained seated as is his wont when visitors of either gender enter his haven.

After Lily got seated at the end of his desk and crossed curvaceous legs, Wolfe asked if she wanted something to drink.

"Would it be gauche to ask for a sherry this long after I have had dinner?"

"Not in this house," Wolfe responded as I went to the cart and found the bottle, pouring a dram of the requested nectar into the proper glass. As I set it down on the small table next to Lily, I got one of those smiles that invariably accelerates my heart rate.

Enough from me. It was time for Wolfe to call the meeting to order.

"Thank you for coming tonight," he said. "One advantage of having both of you in this venture is that you come from different perspectives as far as our missing woman is concerned. Before we continue, Mr. Mason, you need to know what we have learned about Miss Carr's recent financial activity." Wolfe went on to summarize her withdrawal of funds from the bank.

"So, at least fifty grand?" Mason said, exhaling a whistle. "Any idea what the reason is?"

"None at the moment, sir. Let me ask each of you: Does Miss Carr travel frequently, and if so, what are her destinations?"

Lily responded first. "She has always liked the Caribbean—Puerto Rico, Jamaica, the Virgin Islands, Aruba. I don't think there is any one resort she's particularly fond of. She says she likes to try new places down there. Although, come to think of it, I believe that she has stayed in Old San Juan more than once."

"We have never traveled together, either abroad or in the US," Mason put in, "but she has stayed on several occasions at my summer place in the Hamptons, which she likes. And as for trips, she seems partial to Italy, especially the lakes, Como and the others."

"Who wouldn't be?" Lily laughed.

"Has Miss Carr traveled with friends?" Wolfe asked. "And has she ever stayed in facilities owned by acquaintances?"

"She has gone to the islands on occasion with two or three of the women who are in our social group, but no one of them owns a resort home down there."

Wolfe shifted to Mason. "To your knowledge, does she have friends living in the Italian lake country?"

"If she does, she has never mentioned it to me, and I believe she would have."

"Let us move on to Maureen Carr's brother," Wolfe said. "I regret to report that we have learned very little about the man's activities. Miss Rowan already has been given what facts have been unearthed, and, Mr. Mason, I will let Archie tell you what he and our other operatives have found."

I took Mason through my meeting with Alf, Everett Carr's fellow roomer at the Sloane YMCA, as well as our discoveries that Carr was obsessed with betting on the horses and that he was a lousy handicapper.

"A millionaire living at the Y and dressing like a bum?" Mason said. "No wonder Maureen doesn't talk about him."

"We're assuming that he's still a millionaire," I countered, "although the way he seems to be throwing away money on the ponies, his pot of gold may very well have dwindled."

"Have you ever met Everett?" Mason asked Lily.

"No, and Maureen has barely mentioned him to me. I don't know whether she's ashamed of him, or if she simply doesn't know enough about him and what he's doing to have anything to say."

Mason turned to Wolfe. "What are your thoughts?"

"The man clearly has no interest in familial relations or in having anything that resembles a conventional life. We know from this Alf individual and from bookmakers that he has been known to carry large sums on his person, which could make him a robbery target. Also, one who consorts with professional gamblers, that is, bookies, runs the constant risk of hostility."

"You mean if he were to welsh on a bet, for example?" Mason posed.

Wolfe shrugged. "Perhaps. I am not familiar with the niceties of the wagerer, although through the years, Mr. Goodwin and I have run into numerous cases in which gambling debts and other disputes over money have escalated into violence, sometimes with fatal results."

"So you are suggesting that Carr's disappearance may be because of some sort of wager that went bad?"

"I am suggesting nothing, sir, only pointing out the perils associated with gambling. Miss Rowan, do you possess recent photographs of Maureen Carr and her brother?"

"I don't, but I am sure I can get one of Maureen, either from her apartment or from one of the organizations where she is a board member. As for Everett, that's another story altogether. There's a slim chance I might find one at Maureen's apartment. Archie, do you remember if there were photos of either of them when we were at her place?"

"The only shot I remember seeing there was one of her taken years ago, with a middle-aged couple I assume were her parents."

"Why this interest in photographs?" Mason asked.

Wolfe readjusted his bulk. "In addition to Archie, three other operatives in my employ are hunting for Miss Carr and her brother, and each of them needs to be carrying photographs of her as they continue their search."

"I can go to Maureen's apartment tomorrow and hunt for photos of her, and I also will see if I can locate one through one of the agencies where she has been active," Lily said.

"What else should we be doing now?" Mason snapped, pounding a fist into an open palm, a man of action frustrated.

"At present, nothing," Wolfe responded evenly. "I know we all wish to be active, but haste often leads to unwise moves."

The next morning, I was in the office with coffee after breakfast when Lily telephoned. "I got a very good picture of Maureen from Emily Ferris at the orphanage. It's an excellent likeness, taken for use in their current annual report. I had already gone in Maureen's apartment, getting the key from Sofia, who this time did not seem interested in accompanying me. The only shots of Maureen that I found there were years old. And, not surprising, I found no photos of Everett."

"If you will drop by and let me have the pic, I'll have copies made. That's not really a problem, taking a photo of a photo."

The picture Lily gave me later that morning was indeed an excellent likeness of the woman I had met only three times. But I have a good eye for faces, particularly female ones, and I was pleased with what we had. It looked like the shot had been taken within the last year or so. I walked the three blocks to Mel's Camera Shop, which we've used for years for our photographic needs.

"Nice-looking skirt," Mel remarked as he looked at the glossy print that I handed him. "I wouldn't mind knowing this one, Archie. How fast do you need these?"

"As quickly as you can do it. Feel free to bill me double if that helps to speed things up."

Mel waved my comment away. "Nah, you know that we don't pull that kind of stuff here, Archie. You've been a good customer for a long time," he said. "Right now, I'm working on a couple of jobs that came in ahead of you, but I can have these ready in . . . let's see . . . two hours. That okay with you?"

"Plenty okay," I told Mel, and on my return later that afternoon, I got what I needed from him. When Wolfe came down from the plant rooms at six and rang for beer, I had placed one of the prints on his desk blotter. He picked it up, studied it for several seconds, and said, "Adequate."

"I'm glad that you think so. As you know, I have met the woman, and this is her, all right."

Wolfe told me to make sure Saul, Fred, and Orrie each got several copies of the photos and then said, "I would like to see the woman who cleans Miss Carr's home. I believe her name is Sofia. Tonight at nine would be preferable."

I called Lily. "This is my day to discuss business with you. Mr. Wolfe wants to talk to Sofia, in person. Preferably today, at nine p.m."

"I can ask her, although I'm not sure how she will react. She's fairly shy."

"It didn't seem to overly bother her to meet me, did it?"

"No, but you were with me at the time, which made you legitimate, so to speak."

"I have always wanted to be legitimate. Well, I am sure you can persuade Sofia that Nero Wolfe is not some two-headed monster who eats young women for dinner."

"You have such a colorful way of putting things, which must be why I am drawn to you. I will call her and report back."

Next, I phoned our "three musketeers," saying their assignments now extended beyond the search for Everett to include his sister, and that we had pictures of her for them.

"All well and good, Archie, but where are we supposed to be looking for this Maureen Carr?" Orrie asked.

"If the lady has fled town within the last two to three weeks, which is a strong possibility, obvious places to start are Grand Central and Penn stations, the bus terminal, the ferries, LaGuardia, and the North River Piers, where the ocean liners berth. I'm sure Saul can put together a program. Maureen is a good-looking creature, as you will see when you get photographs, and people—particularly men—have an unerring way of remembering such women."

Orrie grumbled about looking for a needle in a haystack, but his complaint was half-hearted, and he said he would stop by for his photographs.

The ever-dependable Lily telephoned just as I hung up with Orrie. "I talked to Sofia, and as I predicted, she's chary about meeting Nero Wolfe."

"*Chary*—now that's Wolfe-type word. Mark me down as impressed."

"You know very well that I have a college degree, and my major was English. I do know my way around a dictionary and a thesaurus."

"Of course you do, I've never doubted it. But back to Sofia: Did you do some arm-twisting?"

"I felt I might have to," Lily said. "I wore her down, though, and she said she would come to the brownstone, but only on the condition that I would accompany her."

"That seems like a reasonable request, and I know Wolfe won't mind. After all, he is moderately comfortable with you."

"I am flattered, knowing as I do his overall attitude about females in his sanctum sanctorum."

"Sanctum sanctorum—there you go again, showing off your education."

"Just reminding you that I am a force to be reckoned with."

"Once again, I have never doubted it. Just don't try to show off in front of Nero Wolfe, or he will brand you a poseur."

"On that note, I will take my leave and will see you and your boss tonight with Sofia in tow."

# CHAPTER 11

I told Wolfe that Lily had gotten Sofia to overcome her reluctance and would deliver her to us. He nodded his approval and then returned to his book. Heaven forbid that the man should have to expend energy by exercising his vocal cords.

Other than the upcoming 9:00 p.m. meeting, the only other activity that day relating to the case was when Saul, Fred, and Orrie dropped by together to pick up photographs of Maureen. Similar to the suggestion I had made to Orrie earlier, Saul had drawn up a plan in which each of the three of them would be assigned to canvass a specific location, such as Penn Station. Sure, this plan was a long shot at best, but we did not have a lot else going for us.

Lily, with Sofia in tow, rang the doorbell at eight fifty-five, and as usual I acted as greeter. "Hello, sir," Sofia said to me, wearing a somber expression and looking like she would rather be anywhere but at an old brownstone on West Thirty-Fifth Street.

I put their coats on the hall hanger and led them into the

office, where at my direction Lily took the red leather chair and Sofia sat primly on the front edge of one of the yellow ones that faced the unoccupied desk. Within seconds, Wolfe walked in, detoured around said desk, and sat. If Sofia was surprised by his bulk, she did not show it. But Lily surely had prepared her for the experience of meeting him.

Once seated, Wolfe dipped his head in his guests' direction, then asked if Sofia and Lily would like something to drink. They both declined.

"Thank you very much for sparing the time to come here tonight, madam," Wolfe said. "I will try not to take too long." Sofia nodded but said nothing.

"How long have you been in Miss Carr's employ?"

"Almost three years."

"You must know her quite well then. Would you say she is a good person to work for?"

"Yes . . . a very nice lady, very nice."

"Does she travel a good deal?"

"Maybe . . . two times a year, maybe three sometimes."

"When Miss Carr does leave home, where does she go, Mrs. Jurek? Does she have favorite locations where she takes vacations?"

Sofia frowned, as if thinking. "She often likes to go to places where it is warm. When she comes home, she is . . . brown."

"Ah, tanned, I see," Wolfe said. "How long is she gone on these trips?"

Another frown. "Two weeks, sometimes longer."

"And does she always tell you when she will be going away?"

"Oh yes, always."

"But not this time, Mrs. Jurek?"

"No . . . not this time," she replied in a subdued voice and shook her head.

"Do you have any idea at all where she might have gone on this occasion?"

"No, I have told them"—she looked at Lily and then at me—"that she did not say anything to me about going away. I am very worried about Miss Carr."

"A natural reaction," Wolfe said. "Did she take a lot of clothing with her?"

"She has so many clothes. Miss Rowan and I went through her closets, but we could not tell how much was missing." She looked at Lily, who nodded and smiled.

"Had Miss Carr ever been married?"

"Yes . . . before I began working for her."

"Have you ever met her former husband?"

Sofia shook her head. It was clear that this questioning was difficult for her, but Wolfe pushed on.

"In the days before Miss Carr disappeared, did you notice any changes in her mood?"

"*Mood . . .* I do not know that word."

"Her behavior. Did she seem different in any way? You have been around Miss Carr a good deal over the last three years, so you must be familiar with how she acts, how she behaves."

Sofia was silent for close to a half minute. When she spoke, it was once again in a voice that could barely be heard. "The last time I saw her, she seemed the same, although maybe a little quieter."

"Would you say that she was sad?"

"I don't . . . think so. Just quiet, like she was thinking."

"Who would you say Miss Carr's best friends are?"

"Miss Rowan is one," she said, turning to Lily. "And Miss Evans and Mrs. Hart."

"That would be Donna Evans and Cordelia Hart," Lily put in. "They are part of a group Maureen and I are in, and I have talked to both of them about Maureen's disappearance. They are every bit as puzzled as I am."

"I believe you were present during some of the social events at Miss Carr's residence."

"Yes, sir. I helped to serve the food and the drinks," Sofia answered.

"Are you collecting Miss Carr's mail for her?" Wolfe asked.

"Yes, I am."

"Have you opened any of it?"

Sofia jerked upright as if she had been slapped. "No! I would never do that!"

"Tell me about the mail."

She gave a sort of shrug, or really more a hunching, of her narrow shoulders. "I haven't looked at any of it," she said in a defensive tone.

"Some of that mail may be important to Miss Carr, or important in finding her," Wolfe said. "I suggest you give all of it to Miss Rowan. You trust her, don't you?"

"Yes, but . . ."

"But what?"

Sofia clenched small fists and shivered. I felt the young woman was getting stretched to the limit of her endurance. "All right . . . Miss Rowan can take all of the mail," she said.

"We are not going to open that mail, Mrs. Jurek, just study it. Do you have any other thoughts about what might have caused Miss Carr to leave home so abruptly?" Wolfe asked.

Realizing she was nearing the end of what she felt was an ordeal, Sofia exhaled and seemed to relax slightly. "No, sir, I do not have any other thoughts about . . . about what has happened to Miss Carr. I am sorry that I cannot be of help."

Wolfe rose without a word and walked out of the office as Sofia watched him with puzzlement. "Another of your boss's abrupt exits," Lily remarked. "He's famous for them, of course."

"If famous is the right word," I replied. "Mrs. Jurek, I echo Mr. Wolfe's thanks for your coming here. You were most patient."

"Sofia, if you go to the hall and get your coat, I'll be along shortly," Lily said. "I need to talk to Mr. Goodwin." The young woman couldn't get out of the office fast enough, and as she exited, Lily turned to me.

"Seems to me that he was a little rough on her," she observed, "or maybe curt is a better word."

"Tact has never been one of Wolfe's strong suits," I conceded, "as you well know."

"And on top of that, he did not get much out of Sofia, as far as I could tell."

"Agreed. I don't think there was a lot of gold to be mined there. Will you get Maureen's mail for us?"

"I will, although I'm not sure how any of it will help us find her."

"Neither am I, but it can't hurt to take a look at it—unopened, of course."

"You will have it tomorrow," Lily said. "And we should bring Eric Mason up to speed on this development, or lack of a development. After all, he is a client, and the paying one, at that."

"We will reach out to Mason," I told her as I walked her to the hall, where Sofia was nervously waiting to get sprung.

# CHAPTER 12

The next morning, Lily called and said she was coming over with Maureen's mail. I then called Eric Mason and filled him in on Sofia's visit to the brownstone and Wolfe's interrogation of her.

"I really should have been present," the ad man had grumped.

"You would have found the evening to be a colossal waste of time. One thing Wolfe requested at that time was to get Maureen's mail, which has been stacking up at her place. Lily Rowan is bringing it here this morning. You're welcome to come over when we take a look at it, although we don't plan to open it."

"When is Lily coming to your place?"

"At eleven, the same time Mr. Wolfe comes into the office from the plant rooms."

"I will be there."

* * *

Mason and Lily arrived within a minute of each other, and both were seated in the office when Wolfe came in, eyed both of them, placed a raceme of yellow *Odontoglossum* in the vase on his desk, and rang for beer.

"I have brought Maureen's mail," Lily told him from the red leather chair, which Mason had graciously insisted she take. "It's in this paper bag," she said as she handed it to Wolfe.

"I had expected more," he said, opening the bag, pulling a two-inch-high pile of items out, and stacking them on his blotter.

Wolfe riffled through them. "A probable statement from Continental Bank and Trust, fat sales flyers from four stores, including Saks and Bloomingdale's, likely invoices from Saks and Lord and Taylor, and envelopes bearing the return addresses of a number of charities, including Breast Cancer Research, Women's Rights Organization, and a Manhattan orphanage."

"Maureen is on the boards of all those groups," Lily said, "and these probably are notifications of upcoming meetings. In fact, there *was* a meeting of the WRO last week that I attended, and Maureen's absence was remarked on because she so rarely misses attending these sessions."

Wolfe scowled and pushed the mail aside as if it were contaminated. "Nothing here adds to our knowledge concerning Miss Carr's whereabouts, although I had suspected this was what Archie calls a long shot." He turned to Lily. "Nonetheless, you should continue to monitor the woman's mail, and you can return this batch to her residence."

I knew Wolfe was at a loss and was flailing about, which is never a pretty sight. Lily and Eric Mason rose to leave, and I escorted them down the hall. "It seems like we're at a dead end," Mason said in a dejected tone. "I'm supposed to have a creative mind, but I'll be damned if I have any suggestions as to what we should be doing next."

"I feel exactly the same way," Lily added in a tone meant to mollify the advertising whiz. "I can't remember ever being this frustrated."

"The good news is," I told them, "that Nero Wolfe does not have the word *surrender* in his vocabulary. I realize the situation at the moment seems bleak, but we've been in worse spots than this before, and he invariably pulls the proverbial rabbit out of the hat." I knew I sounded like a cheerleader trying to exude a confidence I did not at the moment possess.

They both must have sensed my underlying doubts, because neither of them seemed cheered by my little sermon as they left the brownstone wearing somber expressions.

When I got back to the office, Wolfe was in the process of cradling his telephone receiver. I gave him a questioning look, and he said, "I have just given Saul an assignment, and it may be of some help to us. I am a lackwit for not thinking of it before this."

When he shared with me the subject of his conversation with Saul Panzer, I was inclined to agree that he was a lackwit, but then, that made me one as well. And Wolfe told me that Saul was himself chagrined.

Speaking of Saul, he knows well the daily schedule at the brownstone, so it was not surprising that he telephoned, saying he wanted to stop by at six, which is of course when Wolfe rides the elevator down from the plant rooms. "I have got some atoning to do, and the sooner the better," he told me.

Saul already was ensconced in the red leather chair with the scotch I had poured him when Wolfe strode into the office after the afternoon session with those ten thousand orchids up on the roof.

"I have been a ninnyhammer, to use a word of yours," Saul told him.

"No more than Archie and me," replied Wolfe, who has always felt that Saul could do no wrong.

"Nonetheless, I have not been using the brain that Mrs. Panzer gifted me with all of those decades ago. Today, however, I have gotten lucky beyond anything I have a right to deserve."

"Please continue," Wolfe urged as Fritz entered the office with two bottles of beer and a frosted stein on a tray.

"I went to the sedate Park Avenue tower where Maureen Carr resides, and who should I find as the doorman but none other than Seamus Rafferty."

"I have met him," I put in.

"Don't interrupt, Archie," Wolfe said, holding up a palm and turning to Saul. "Please continue."

"I had occasion to run into Rafferty some years back when he was about to find himself in big trouble. He was a grifter running short cons and was working the old shell game on a Lower East Side street corner. I had learned from another freelance dick that the cops were planning a major raid on the cons who were running rampant in the neighborhood. I happened to walk by Rafferty, who was at work on some sucker and I told him that he had better close up shop, which he did. And wouldn't you know that fifteen minutes later, a patrol car came by and nailed another grifter, who was working three-card monte on some sucker in the very same block.

"Rafferty was grateful to me. He was so thankful that he insisted on buying me drinks at a nearby saloon, which I of course accepted. 'I will never forget this,' he told me. 'Any time I can help you, just ask.'"

"So he ended up going straight," I said.

"Yeah, that's one piece of good news. Another is that he has an extremely good memory, and when I walked up to him on Park Avenue today, he spoke my name and wanted to throw his arms around me."

"Very touching," I remarked dryly.

"Don't worry, Archie, I didn't let him hug me. But I took him up on that offer he had made way back when. I told him I was working for a close relative of Maureen Carr, and that this relative is terribly worried about her whereabouts. I asked if he had seen her leave home sometime in the last three weeks with a suitcase and he said no, but one of the other doormen might have."

"How many of these sentinels are there?" Wolfe asked.

"During the week, three, who each work eight-hour shifts, plus relief men who come in on weekends. Seamus gave me their telephone numbers, and my luck held as I managed to reach all of them, including at least one who I probably woke up. I struck out on the first three calls, including the graveyard shift man, who said he couldn't remember Maureen Carr leaving at any time on his watch, and the same with the weekend men. But I hit paydirt with the evening guy, named Henry, who works four to midnight. He remembered getting a cab for Maureen about four thirty p.m. about a month ago but he can't remember the date."

"Did she have luggage?"

"Yes, just a single suitcase, which suggests a short trip. Henry thinks he heard her tell the cabbie to take her to Grand Central, but again, he can't recall for sure."

"Where do trains go when they leave Grand Central?" I stipulate that Wolfe is a genius, but yawning gaps exist in his knowledge, including the country's current transportation system. He probably cannot name a major railroad, airline, or bus system.

"Its trains run mostly west," Saul said in answer to Wolfe's query. "They go as far as Chicago and St. Louis, as well as to hundreds of places in between. Given the time Miss Carr was picked up, she could have been taking the Pacemaker, which leaves here at three."

"The Pacemaker?" Wolfe raised his eyebrows.

"Oh, sorry, Mr. Wolfe. The Pacemaker, final destination, Chicago."

"Whom do you have covering Grand Central?" Wolfe asked.

"Fred. I'll have him show Miss Carr's picture around. It's an unlikely bet, but somebody might remember her."

The unlikely bet paid off, at least to a degree. Fred called the next morning to tell me he had some news. "I can bring it at eleven," he said.

Fred Durkin has always been in awe of Wolfe, and he's like the hardworking, earnest kid in grade school who desires nothing more than to please his teacher. He knows very well when Wolfe begins his working day in the office, so picking that time to show up at the brownstone was not an accident.

Fred already was parked in one of the yellow chairs when Wolfe entered the office, greeted him, and reached down to press the button in the leg-hole of his desk as a signal to Fritz. "Will you join me in having a beer?" Wolfe asked.

"Yes, sir," was the response from Fred, who may or may not like beer, but as I have reported, he always has one with Wolfe because he thinks that it's the thing to do.

After they both were settled with their drinks, Wolfe said, "Archie tells me you learned something while at Grand Central Terminal."

"Yes, sir, I did. Saul had told me that Maureen Carr took a taxi from home to the station a while back—he did not know the exact date—but it would have been at a time of day when the Pacemaker was preparing to leave. I timed it yesterday so that I got there when she would have, and I managed to talk my way onto the Pacemaker's platform when the passengers were boarding.

"I had the picture of Miss Carr and showed it to a couple of conductors, asking if they recognized her, but they just shrugged and walked away from me. Then I saw a redcap who had delivered bags to one of the cars and was coming toward me with his empty two-wheeled cart. 'Do you recognize this woman?' I asked him.

"He looked at the photo, looked at it some more, squinting, and said, 'Yeah, I do. I carried her bag some time back, and what I remember, besides her being very pretty, was how friendly she was to me. Most of the folks who take this train, they're rich, and they let you know it—maybe she's loaded, too—but they are not nice, not polite, at least not to me, they aren't. They act like big shots. But her, she asked me how my day was going and made it seem like she really meant it. She also gave me a bigger tip than she needed to, but that's not what I remember most about her, it's the way she treated me.'"

"Was there anything else the redcap had to tell you about her?"

"Yes, Mr. Wolfe. He told me she acted like she was sad about something, but of course he didn't know what. Also, he said that from what he could tell, she was going only as far as Albany, which he said seems strange for someone riding a train that runs all the way west to Chicago. There are other, cheaper New York Central trains that she could have taken to Albany."

"Satisfactory, Fred."

Durkin flushed and smiled at the praise. If he knew how rarely Nero Wolfe doles out that word, his grin would have been even wider.

# CHAPTER 13

"Well, we now know a little more about Maureen Carr than before," I said to Wolfe. "Your thoughts?"

"Why would she go to Albany, if that is where she really went? Do you see any significance in that?"

"Other than that it's the state capital, I have no idea. I've only passed through, and it's not a very large burg. I don't know the population, but it would be a lot smaller if you subtracted all the politicians."

Wolfe scowled at my attempt at humor and began going through the morning mail that I had stacked on his blotter.

"Now that we've learned by which route Maureen left town, shouldn't I have Saul call off the boys—and himself? No need to be watching stations and airports anymore. And the expenses are piling up."

"Yes, by all means, have them stop. I am sure we will have chores for them later."

\* \* \*

That afternoon, when Wolfe was up in the plant rooms with Theodore Horstmann, and I was logging in orchid germination records in the office, the phone rang. "Nero Wolfe's office, Archie Goodwin speaking."

"I want to speak to Nero Wolfe—and right now!" a hoarse voice rasped.

"I'm sorry, Mr. Wolfe is not available at the moment. Who is calling?"

"I will tell you who's calling—it is Stanley Jurek, that's who, and I want to talk to this Wolfe character about the way he treated my wife!"

Wolfe may indeed be a character, although I have never heard him called that. "I'm sorry, Mr. Jurek, but as I said, Mr. Wolfe is not available at the present time. In what way did he mistreat your wife?"

"He browbeat her, goddamn it, that's what. And he is going to answer to me for it."

"I will give Mr. Wolfe the message. May I have your telephone number?"

"Here are two, at work and at home," he said, reading them off. "I had better hear from him today, got that, Mister Whatever-your-name-is? And remember this: I know where he lives."

When Wolfe returned from his orchid playtime at six, I gave him Jurek's message, verbatim.

"I would like to meet this gentleman."

"Based on my brief conversation with him, I believe you are stretching the definition of that description. But I quibble. When would you like to see him?"

"Tonight, at nine."

I reached Jurek at home, and he was still exorcised. "Tonight? That's damned short notice!"

"You sounded most anxious to meet Mr. Wolfe, which I made clear to him. If you want to see him, tonight is the time. Take it or leave it."

Jurek swore, twice, but he said he would be at the brownstone and slammed down his receiver. Next, I did something Wolfe would not have liked, but among my many duties, explicit or otherwise, is to keep the man safe. For that reason, I made a telephone call.

The doorbell made its noise at 8:57 p.m. by my watch, which is never more than fifteen seconds off. I did the honors, first looking through the one-way glass. Jurek was thick all over—not fat, but thick. He was an inch taller than me and easily twenty-five pounds heavier. He had just begun to go to fat in the middle, but he still looked like he would hold his own in a barroom brawl.

"Mr. Jurek, you are right on time," I said as I swung open the front door. He stormed in without a word and whipped off his raincoat. "I'll hang that up," I said, maintaining a cordial tone, even though he looked like he was going to start growling. "This way to the office," I said as we walked down the hall to the office. I was pleased to note that as we went by, the door to the front room was ajar.

Jurek bulled his way into the office and looked around. "Where's Wolfe?" he demanded.

"He'll be in shortly," I said, gesturing him to the red leather chair, which he plopped into. "Can I get you something to drink?"

"No! I didn't come here to socialize. I am—" He stopped in midsentence as Wolfe walked in and detoured around his desk, taking a seat.

"Geez, you're, you're . . ."

"Fat, Mr. Jurek? That is patently obvious. Would you like something to drink? I will be having beer."

"I already made the offer, and he passed," I said.

"Just so. Mr. Goodwin said you asked to see me."

Jurek lifted halfway out of the chair. "You bullied my wife right here, and you are going to pay for that!"

"Indeed, sir? And just how did I bully her, to use your word?"

"You treated her like she was some sort of a crime suspect, with all of your questions. She came home a nervous wreck."

"I am sorry to hear that. I treated her with the utmost civility. As you are aware, your wife's employer, Maureen Carr, is missing, and we are investigating her disappearance."

"That doesn't give you the right to make Sofia seem like she's some kind of suspect, and I said you'll pay!" Before I could react, Jurek stood up and leaned across Wolfe's desk, thick arms out, reaching for him.

"Hey, get back, what the hell do you think you're—" Jurek spun around and grabbed me in an armlock and began to squeeze as I pummeled his soft midsection and yelled "Geronimo!" Within seconds, the aggressor's arms lost their strength and he groaned, but it wasn't just from my punches. When I spun away, I saw and heard Fred Durkin, who put a full nelson on our visitor and was exerting pressure. "Stop fighting me or I'll make it plenty worse, pal," Fred said.

"Get away from me, damn it!" the man yowled, but Fred didn't let go of him until he had collapsed into the red leather chair amid swearing and more yowls of pain.

"Enough, Fred," said Wolfe, who had his beer stein cocked in his right hand, ready to hurl it as he rolled his chair backward to get away from the lunge. "I believe the gentleman now comprehends the situation."

Durkin retreated to a corner of the office but crouched as if to pounce and kept his narrowed eyes on the slumped Jurek, who was still groaning and testing his arms to see if they still functioned. "Sorry, Mr. Wolfe, I didn't mean to hurt him. I used to be a boxer, not a wrestler, and maybe I just got carried away."

"Who said you hurt me?" Jurek snarled. "You blindsided me, that's what. Sneaking up from behind like that. I would've mashed you if we were face-to-face."

"There are occasions when it is prudent to concede defeat, sir," Wolfe said. "This is one of those occasions."

Jurek swore again, but his words had lost much of their force. "Can I get you a drink?" I asked him for the second time.

"Uh . . . yeah, okay, how 'bout a rye on the rocks?" Going to the liquor table, I did the honors and told Fred I felt conditions were under control and that he could return to the front room.

"Now, sir," Wolfe said, smoothing his hair, "are you ready to continue our discussion?"

"I don't see that we have anything to discuss other than your treatment of my wife."

"I disagree. When you chose to interrupt our conversation, I was about to ask you if you have met Miss Carr."

"Yeah, a few times, and so what?" Jurek said as he took a healthy swig of his drink.

"Do you feel she has been a good employer to your wife?"

"I guess," he replied with a shrug. "Be nice if Maureen paid her better—hell, she's got the dough."

"Did your wife request higher wages?"

He waved the question away. "Nah, Sofia is just too shy, too meek. I told her she should ask for a raise, but she didn't want to. She's never been very assertive."

"I understand you met her in England during the war."

"Not that it is any of your business, but I did. She was a DP from Poland, and the Brits took her in, along with a lot of others like her."

"A most admirable stance by one of our wartime Allies," Wolfe remarked. "Did you see combat during the war?"

"Did I? Hell yes—I was with Patton's Third Army in '44 as we barreled across Germany. By then I'd been promoted to master sergeant," he said, puffing his chest out. "What a bloody time that was, lots of hand-to-hand combat along the way. I went up against one Jerry near Oppenheim and shot the bastard dead."

"You are owed our gratitude for your service, sir," Wolfe said. "Switching back to the present, it would seem she has adjusted well to life in the United States."

"She has, and why shouldn't she? Sofia is no dummy, I knew that from the first time I met her."

"You are a perceptive individual," Wolfe said. "Do you have any idea as to why Miss Carr has disappeared?"

"No, I don't, and this is sounding like what you did with Sofia, grilling her."

"I did not grill your wife, to use a police term, nor am I grilling you. I am merely probing. And I should think both you and she should be concerned about Miss Carr's whereabouts, first as caring people, and second, albeit less important, because the woman is a source of income for your family."

That seemed to stymie Jurek, but he was still in a pout, with his arms folded across his chest. "We'll get along one way or another."

"I understand you work in the scrap metal business."

"It's a living, and I'm with a company I started with before I went to war."

"There is something to be said for job security," Wolfe acknowledged. "I assume you are happy there."

"Yeah. Anything else you want to know?"

"Not at the moment. If either you or your wife hear from Miss Carr, or learn where she is, I would appreciate you telling me."

Jurek didn't respond, just slugged back the rest of his drink, stood up, and headed for the office door with me not far behind. No words were exchanged as I followed him down the hall, gave him his coat, and closed the front door behind him, locking it. When I got back to the office, Wolfe had just picked up a book as I said, "So much for Mr. Personality."

That was met with what I would best describe as a snort. "How did Fred happen to be here?" he demanded.

"It was my idea. Call it a premonition, but I didn't like the sound of Jurek over the phone, and I felt there might be trouble, so I arranged for backup."

Another snort. "I did not realize Fred had been a boxer."

"As an amateur only. He had been in Golden Gloves tournaments years ago. To hear him tell it, he wasn't bad, but said he just got tired of getting hit and knew he wasn't good enough to become a professional."

"When did you smuggle him in here?"

"I would hardly term it 'smuggling,' but it was while you were in the kitchen with Fritz."

"And what was this nonsense with the word *Geronimo*?"

"That was a prearranged signal. Fred was in the front room with the door slightly open when Jurek came in. If he heard me speak that word, he was to come to the office—as he did."

"And why did you invoke the name of the most famous of Apache tribal leaders?"

"Just caprice on my part. It's a word that US paratroops use when they jump out of planes."

Wolfe looked like he could chew nails. "Is Fred still here?"

"He's in the front room."

"Pay him one hundred dollars."

"What about Mr. Jurek?"

"It is safe to assume we have not heard the last of the man," Wolfe said as he rose and walked out of the office.

# CHAPTER 14

The next morning as I was at my desk with coffee after breakfast, Wolfe called from his bedroom. "Telephone Saul," he said,
"and see if he can be here this morning at eleven."

"Do I tell him what it's about?"

"No, we will leave that until he is here," Wolfe said, hanging up
abruptly. The man has never learned phone etiquette and never
will. I reached Saul Panzer on the first try, and he also was curious
as to the reason for the summons, but I told him he would just
have to wait, because I was in the dark, as is often the case.

Panzer had planted himself in the red leather chair with a cup of
coffee when Wolfe walked in and rang for beer. "Thank you for
coming, Saul. How well do you know Albany?"

"Not very. Oh, I've been there a few times, including one for-
gettable occasion when I did a job for a longtime state senator
who said he was being followed and wanted me to find out who

was dogging him. I ended up spending a cold night on dark Albany streets trailing the guy who was trailing the senator."

"Don't leave us in suspense. What happened?" I asked.

"Turned out the stalker, a hardware salesman, had been on wild goose chase. He thought the senator was having an affair with his wife, but when I got them to meet face-to-face, the cuckold realized he had followed the wrong man and apologized profusely. I was paid, but given my time plus the travel, the assignment was only barely profitable."

"I hope the experience in that city has not soured you on the possibility of revisiting it," Wolfe said.

"As Bugs Bunny might say, 'I'm all ears,'" Saul responded.

If anyone else had delivered that line, Wolfe would have reacted with a scowl or a *pfui*, but given the esteem with which he holds Saul Panzer, he did not react. "As you know, we have learned through Fred that Maureen Carr took a train to Albany and has not been heard from or seen since."

"Yeah, good work on his part, not that I'm surprised. I'm guessing you want me to hunt the lady down."

"Your guess is correct. Do you see any impediments to such an undertaking?"

Saul shrugged. "The good news is that Albany is not all that big. Armed with a photo of Miss Carr, I can easily canvass the downtown hotels, and outlying ones as well, if needed. The bad news is twofold: one, we don't know if she even stayed in a hotel; and two, it has been more than three weeks since she hopped that train north, so she might not even be in Albany anymore. But I've faced worse obstacles before, so I am ready to go."

"Excellent. Archie, do you have anything to add?"

"Saul's pretty well covered the situation. I'll give Lily a call, though, just to find out whether she knows if Maureen has any friends or connections in Albany."

"I can take a train up there today," Saul said.

Wolfe nodded his approval and I called Lily, who said she knew no one or nothing to connect Maureen Carr to our state capital.

We did not hear from Saul until the next day, when he telephoned while Wolfe was having his afternoon session with the orchids. "I now can write a guidebook about the lobbies of Albany's hotels," he said, "although I wouldn't bet on what kind of sales it would get. On the fifth place I visited, which is probably the best one in town, the desk clerk immediately recognized Miss Carr's picture."

"So she stayed there?"

"Right, Archie, for a grand total of two nights."

"Did she use her own name when she checked in?"

"I'm getting to that. I asked to see the guest register, and, no surprise, I was told rather primly that peeking at that sacred book was against the hotel's regulations. But the double sawbuck I slid across the counter to the clerk overrode those regulations as well as that primness. Our lady did indeed check into room 419 as Maureen Carr of New York City, and she checked out at noon on the third day.

"I then asked if she had visitors or got any telephone calls, and because the Andrew Jackson I had given the clerk still had wheels, he told me, albeit reluctantly, that a man had come into the lobby, and that he and the woman who'd registered as Maureen Carr left the hotel, and that she returned later—about an hour and a half later—the clerk thought. He described the man to me as 'fiftyish, rather short, thin, well dressed, and balding.' In answer to the question that you are about to ask, he said he'd never seen the man before."

"Well, that's something of a start. Got anything more to add?"

"The desk clerk, still impressed by the double sawbuck, introduced me to the switchboard operator, who said she had no record of the guest in 419 receiving any calls, and then he put me in touch with the bellhop, who remembered Maureen."

"Did he also know anything about the man who came to pick up her up?"

"Like the clerk, he said he had never seen the guy before. But he did tell me that the next day, after she had checked out, he hailed a cab for her, and she took it to, of all places, the railroad station."

"Which means she could either have got a train south down the Hudson, in the direction of New York City, or west, in the direction of Chicago."

"You must have gotten good grades in geography," Saul said.

"In high school, I memorized the names of all the Ohio counties, and in alphabetical order no less."

"Okay, serves me right for bringing up the subject. Do I need to report to Wolfe, or can I trust you to accurately deliver the information to him?"

"When can you take the next rattler back?"

"Funny you should ask. I'm at the Albany depot right now, and a southbound express, not a rattler, is due in fifteen minutes. The trip takes just over three hours."

"Which means you should get in by a little before nine. When you get in, give me a call from Grand Central. Instructions to follow. And go easy on the drinks in the bar car."

"Wow, spoken like an executive. I'm impressed."

"As well you should be."

When Wolfe descended, I told him Saul could be here to report after our dinner of pork tenderloin in casserole. He dipped his chin an eighth of an inch in approval, rang for beer, and dove into his latest book, *Berlin Diary*, by William L. Shirer.

Saul phoned when we were in the office with coffee, and I told him to come ahead and said I would give him a scotch if he hadn't overimbibed on the train.

Saul must have wanted that scotch badly, because he rang the doorbell twelve minutes later. "The bar car was too raucous for my taste," he said as he came in and peeled off his coat. "A bunch of commuting types from Upstate who couldn't wait to begin celebrating the end of the workweek. I retired to a quiet coach with a newspaper."

"Good evening, Saul," Wolfe said as he dog-eared a page in his book and set it down. "I hope your trip was not too onerous."

"I survived it, sir," Saul responded and nodded his thanks when I handed him a scotch. "I am not proud of my results in Albany. You probably should have sent someone else."

"I will be the judge of that," Wolfe said. "Proceed."

Saul gave the same summary I had heard from him, with one addition. "Just before I boarded the train back to Grand Central, I showed the ticket agent in the Albany station the picture of Maureen and gave him the date and the approximate time she would have been in the depot.

"'Nope, I was here all that day, and I didn't see her,' the agent said, handing the photo back. 'And I sure as heck would have remembered the face.'"

"What does that tell you?" Wolfe asked.

"One of two things. That Maureen paid for her ticket on the train going south out of Albany, or she had bought a round-trip fare at Grand Central."

"You like to give odds, Saul. Where was she going?"

"Twenty to one, south from Albany. What's to the west? Syracuse? Rochester? Buffalo? Even Chicago? I see her going only south, getting off somewhere in Westchester County, possibly, or much more likely, back to New York."

Wolfe turned to me. "Might she have returned to her residence?"

"Hard to believe," I said. "Lily has been calling her number every three hours for days, without a response. Oh, I suppose it's possible she's there and isn't answering her phone, but that seems unlikely. Want me to go and take a look?"

"Not yet," Wolfe said, "although we may call upon Miss Rowan soon to investigate. Does either of you have a theory as to why Miss Carr went to Albany?"

"Beats me," Saul said. "Archie, you are said to be an expert on attractive women and their foibles. Any thoughts?"

"I don't know who credited me with such expertise, but whatever insights I am supposed to have about the fairer sex have been greatly overrated, as Lily will be only so happy to point out. I pass."

"I am at a loss as well," Saul said. "Miss Carr's trip to Albany left us with more questions than answers."

Wolfe drew in air and exhaled. "Archie, we need to keep our clients apprised of the latest developments—Mr. Jurek's rancorous visit and Miss Carr's decamping to Albany and her subsequent evaporation. Can you arrange to have them here tomorrow at eleven a.m.?"

Arrange I did. Lily said she was anxious for the opportunity to get caught up, while Mason grumped that he should have heard from us sooner.

When our clients arrived at the brownstone the next morning, their moods of the previous day had not changed. Lily was eager and questioning, while Eric Mason crossed his arms over his chest and stewed. Wolfe entered the room, detoured around his desk, and favored our guests with the slightest of bows.

"Will either of you have something to drink, coffee perhaps? Fritz has brewed a fresh pot." Lily said yes to coffee, Mason shook his head.

"I have asked Mr. Panzer to be present with us this morning, as he, along with the two of us, have some developments to report, although you will not find them to be wholly satisfactory."

"I hope I haven't come here for nothing," Mason said.

"I echo that hope," Wolfe replied. "Let us begin with a visit paid here by Stanley Jurek, Sofia's husband, a couple of days ago."

"That must have been interesting," Lily said.

"There are myriad definitions of *interesting*, Miss Rowan," Wolfe responded. "I will leave it to you to determine which of them best describes the situation. The gentleman was less than pleased with me because of his contention that my questioning of his wife was overzealous and demeaning. He vigorously disputed my version of events, became violent, and had to be forcibly restrained."

"Bravo to Archie!" Lily said, clapping.

"No, bravo to Fred Durkin," I corrected her.

"Back to Mr. Jurek," Wolfe said. "He entered this office unhappy, and he left it unhappy. Also, he seemed to have little interest in Miss Carr's disappearance. Has either of you had occasion to meet him?"

"Not me," Mason said. "I've only met Sofia once, when I picked Maureen up to go to the theater. And we only exchanged a few words."

"I've never met Mr. Jurek, and I have seen Sofia several times," Lily put in. "She has often served drinks and hors d'oeuvres at gatherings of our women's groups. But like Eric, I have barely spoken to her. She seems pleasant but shy and is very self-effacing."

"That would be natural," Wolfe said, "given the duties she is asked to perform in her employer's residence. Now we come to a trip Miss Carr has taken."

That got the attention of Lily and Mason, and they started talking over each other with their shocked questions. "Please!" Wolfe said, silencing the cacophony, turning to Saul, and saying, "You will want to hear from Mr. Panzer."

Saul proceeded to describe his encounter with the doorman at Maureen's building that led to his learning that a taxi had taken her to Grand Central a while back.

"That was lucky," Mason remarked.

"Mr. Panzer has a way of making events appear to be lucky," Wolfe remarked, nodding to Saul to continue.

"The real credit goes to Fred Durkin, whose name you heard a couple of minutes ago," Saul said. "Given the time of day that Miss Carr headed for the big station, I had guessed she might have taken the Twentieth Century Limited. Armed with her photo, Fred followed up and found a redcap at Grand Central who hauled her bag and remembered she was going to Albany."

"Why would Maureen go to Albany?" Mason asked. "Seems strange."

"Do you have any thoughts, Miss Rowan?" Wolfe posed.

"I'm sorry, but I don't. Maureen and I were in a group that went up there two years ago to appear before a state panel that wanted to learn more about existing facilities in New York for unwed mothers. I recall her saying that it was the first time she had been in Albany."

Wolfe drank beer and dabbed his lips with a handkerchief. "Mr. Panzer has learned a little about Miss Carr's more recent visit to that city." Saul then proceeded to describe his discovery that Maureen had left the hotel with a man said to be "fiftyish, short, balding" and she returned alone an hour and a half later.

"And nobody at the hotel knew anything about this mystery man?" Mason asked.

"Neither the desk clerk nor the bellhop told me they had ever seen him before," Saul replied.

"Did the guy take Maureen away from the hotel in a car?"

"I asked, and nobody had paid any attention to them, or to the car, either, for that matter."

"Why not?" the adman demanded.

"Why should they? No one at the hotel had any reason to be suspicious," Saul said. "For all they knew, it was just a man picking up a woman to go out on a date, dinner maybe. That likely happens all the time."

"Mr. Panzer is right," Lily said. "Neither Maureen nor the mystery man, as Eric refers to him, were known to the staff at the hotel. What would they have to be suspicious about?"

"So it seems that we really haven't learned anything substantive," Mason said, "despite all your efforts." He made a sweeping arm gesture meant to encompass Wolfe, Saul, me, and presumably, the absent Fred Durkin. "Did Maureen leave Albany?"

"She apparently did, that day," Saul replied. "The bellhop put her in a cab to the station. I showed the ticket taker at the depot her picture, and he had no recollection of seeing her board a train, so we're left to assume she went back south, presumably to New York on a round-trip ticket."

"Miss Rowan, I understand you make a telephone call to Maureen Carr's residence every few hours," Wolfe said.

"I do. There is never an answer, obviously, except once when Sofia answered, hoping, so she said, that it might be Maureen. She was there to do dusting, as she has twice a week since Maureen has been . . . gone."

"It is time to again check Miss Carr's mail. Can you see to this?"

"Of course," Lily said. "And I suppose you want me to bring the mail to you?"

"Yes," Wolfe replied. "It will once again remain unopened, but there is a possibility, albeit slim, that something in the post will provide a suggestion as to where she is."

"Sounds like you are really grasping at straws," Mason said.

"Perhaps, sir, but even straws can be helpful in telling which way the wind blows."

"I don't know about the wind, but I'm paying to find out where Maureen is, and I will spend whatever it takes. There ought to be some way for you to find out who she was with in Albany."

"Isn't it possible that Maureen's luncheon partner that day was her own brother?" Lily posed.

"It is, although unlikely," Wolfe replied. "However, your point is well taken. We have neither a photograph nor a description of him. Has Miss Carr ever mentioned his physical appearance?"

"No, not once. I haven't any idea at all about his height, his hair color, whether he wears glasses, nothing whatever," Lily said.

# CHAPTER 15

Both our clients left the brownstone that morning frustrated, but they were hardly alone. The three of us—Wolfe, Saul, and I—were also far from satisfied. For several seconds after their departure, no one spoke. Finally, Wolfe said, "Archie, get Fred and Orrie here at three. Saul, I assume you can also be present at that time."

"Yes, sir, I can."

That was Wolfe at his finger-snapping best. Give an order, and expect it to be carried out, without question. But then, I follow orders—most of the time. In this case, I was able to deliver, and the trio of operatives sat in the office at three with drinks, awaiting direction.

Wolfe summarized the situation, admitting a lack of progress. "We don't know where Maureen Carr is, we don't know where her brother is, and we also don't know the identity of the man Miss Carr met with in Albany, call him Mr. X."

"I wasn't very successful up there," Saul said. "I will pay for that trip myself, to atone for my failure."

"Nonsense!" Wolfe snapped. "You did not have a lot to go on. I would like to learn the identity of Mr. X, which may allow us to break this logjam. I propose, if you are willing, that all three of you go to Albany, armed with photographs of Miss Carr, and spread out, combing the city and its environs.

"Go into establishments there, primarily restaurants and bars, and learn if anyone can identify Mr. X. I concede this is a challenge, but Miss Carr and this man apparently were together for between one and two hours. It is likely they were seen, and it also is likely, although by no means sure, that one of those individuals who observed the pair might be able to identify Miss Carr's escort, who may well be a denizen of Albany. And each of you probably should rent an automobile to assist in your search."

"I'm game," Saul said. "What about you two?"

"Count me in," Durkin answered. "They must have gone someplace to eat—or drink."

"Or both," Orrie chimed in. "Is Archie going, too?"

As I mentioned before, Orrie Cather always has been interested in what my role will be in a case, because he is convinced that he would fit nicely into my role as Wolfe's assistant.

"I have assignments for Archie here, Orrie," Wolfe replied. "I believe the three of you are an adequate force to cover Albany and the surrounding area. I expect daily reports from you, Saul."

"What if we learn the guy's identity? Do we try to find him?" Orrie asked.

"Not yet," Wolfe said. "Telephone for instructions." That settled, the boys departed and Saul said they would leave for Albany that afternoon.

"The expense accounts for this project will be hefty," I told Wolfe.

"So far, these trips have only been to Albany. It is not as if we are putting people on airplanes to California or Florida," he said.

"True. And Eric Mason seems ready and eager to provide whatever funds are needed, so I suppose I shouldn't worry. Do you honestly believe that one among our stalwart trio will learn the identity of our Mr. X?"

"You have said you like long shots, Archie."

"True, it's always entertaining to see a fifty-to-one horse win a race. But I would never bet those odds myself. All right, what do we do now?"

"We wait to look at Miss Carr's mail, another long shot."

Wolfe was frustrated, and so was I, for that matter. But I failed to see how looking at unopened mail could possibly help us. As if on cue, Lily telephoned, and I told Wolfe to pick up his phone. "I have Maureen's mail, Archie. When would you like me to bring it over?"

"I am about to visit the orchids, Miss Rowan, but you can bring it here anytime," Wolfe said.

Lily told us she would come now, which was jake with me. Her presence would give me a lift, and I needed one.

Less than a half hour later, the doorbell rang, and there she was on the stoop, clutching to her chest a shopping bag filled with mail.

"Set it down on Wolfe's desk," I told her when we got to the office. "Did you see Sofia at Maureen's place?"

"I didn't. I had asked her to give me a key so I wouldn't have to pester her every time I went there."

"She had a spare?"

"She does now. She said she was afraid to lose the one she had, so she got two duplicates made at a hardware store and gave one to me. She said she was sure Maureen wouldn't mind."

"Very smart of her."

"I think she *is* very smart, Archie, and I was surprised when she said she was afraid of losing the key. I can't imagine her being that careless. At first, she comes off as shy and humble, self-effacing, as you might say. But the more I've gotten to know her, I have seen an inner strength and a determination to succeed."

"Glad to hear that. She certainly speaks English well."

"Sofia told me that in the time she spent in England during and just after the war, she listened to the people around her and was able to pick up the language quickly."

"That assumes the language the Brits speak is the same one you and I use to communicate."

"*Very* funny, Mr. Goodwin," she said, giving me a mild shove.

"That's me, ever the card. Always leave 'em laughing is my motto."

"Why do you think I was attracted to you in the first place? You've always made me laugh."

"As long as you're laughing *with* me and not *at* me."

"It's really a little of both."

Lily had only been in the brownstone five minutes, and already I was feeling better. That's what she does for me, and to me. "Say, the dinner Fritz is preparing for tonight is such that Wolfe can easily eat all of the entrée. I suggest we have cocktails at the Plaza bar and then sup at Rusterman's. My treat, of course."

"In addition to being funny, you are one sweet talker, as I've often said."

When I got back to the brownstone later that night, Wolfe was still at his desk. "I trust you and Miss Rowan had a pleasant dinner."

"We did, and I knew you wouldn't miss me. I assume you were able to finish tonight's entrée yourself."

"I was. I also went through the latest batch of Miss Carr's mail and found nothing of interest."

"Did the boys, or most likely Saul, check in from Albany?"

"No, but they have only been there a few hours. I expect we will hear from them tomorrow."

Saul did indeed call in the next day, just after Wolfe had come down from his morning excursion in the greenhouse. "Fred seems to be on a hot streak," he said as Wolfe picked up his instrument and I stayed on the line. "He keeps learning more than either Orrie or me."

"Don't keep us in suspense," I said.

"I just want to make sure he gets full credit. Late last night, and I do mean in the wee hours, Fred had been making the rounds of numerous eateries north of Albany when he stopped at a roadhouse on Route 378. He showed Miss Carr's photo around, and one of the waiters recognized her. He remembered she had been in there at lunch a few weeks back with a man named Miles Hirsch."

"What was the waiter able to tell Fred about Mr. Hirsch?" Wolfe asked.

"Not much, other than he'd eaten in the joint several times. This morning, all three of us have been asking around at hotels, restaurants, and shops about Hirsch and haven't had a lot of luck. One counterman Orrie talked to in a coffee shop, though, seemed to know who he was and clammed up tight."

"Spend some more time today making inquiries, Saul," Wolfe said. "But do not beat the proverbial dead horse and return home by nightfall."

I turned to Wolfe after we had cradled our phones. "It is time for a call to Lon Cohen." He nodded in agreement.

I described our relationship with Lon Cohen earlier. He is always curious as to what Wolfe and I are working on, and he would be again this time, so I decided to put him on the defensive. After he answered by barking his name as usual, I said, "Nero Wolfe and I were chatting yesterday and trying to remember how many scoops we've given to the *Gazette*. We came up with—"

"Just a minute, private flatfoot. Why do I feel like you've got your hand in the pocket where I keep my wallet?"

"First, my feet are not flat. Second, my boss and I were just having an academic discussion."

"Academic, my aunt Fannie. It's painfully obvious that you're looking for something, which invariably is the case when you call me. Look, I've got deadlines looming. Out with it—what is it that you want?"

"Does the name Miles Hirsch mean anything to you, Mr. Cohen?" Wolfe asked.

"It does. Why do you need to know?"

"Just curious," I said.

"You two are never 'just curious.' Does this have anything to do with your query a few days back about a man named Everett Carr?" Lon asked.

"It might," I said.

"Of course, it might. I recall that Carr was in a Hell's Kitchen bookie joint during a raid and Miles Hirsch is one of the biggest gamblers in the state, legitimate or otherwise—often otherwise. I am surprised that neither of you have heard of him."

"We are not overly conversant with the world of wagering," I told him.

"Certainly not the kind of wagering you do every Thursday night at Panzer's poker table."

"If I recall correctly, I was the big winner last week, and you were among those who left with fewer shekels than when the evening began."

"Hey, miracles happen. Or as they say, every dog has his day."

"Arf. Now what can you tell me about Miles Hirsch?"

"I'll call you back in five or ten minutes. I've got a couple things I have to deal with right now."

It was thirty minutes later when Lon phoned us. "Okay, I've had the clips on Hirsch brought up from the morgue, and we've written almost nothing about him. I've learned more about the man from a couple of our court and beat reporters. It's apparent that he's one sharp customer. Or maybe it's more accurate to say he's got sharp mouthpieces, because although he's been charged several times, he has always managed to avoid the cooler. He's a big-time operator, with a co-op on Park Avenue and a country place up near Saratoga Springs, where that famous track is. He also owns a string of racehorses, although someone else fronts for him, so his name never appears in connection with the horses."

"Among his activities, is he a moneylender?" Wolfe asked.

That brought a chuckle from Lon. "You might say that. He operates like a big-time bookmaker, and he charges high interest rates to those he makes loans to, according to one of our men. It sounds like this must have something to do with that guy Carr you asked about."

"It might, although we're still feeling our way here," I put in.

"Well, my advice is to feel your way very carefully. I told you Hirsch is sharp, but he's shady as well. He has got some toughs working for him, and they've been known to threaten people who owe him money."

"Has anybody complained about strong-arm stuff?"

"A few have, although Hirsch usually talks his way out of trouble—with his lawyers' help. Apparently, the threats are subtle enough that they're hard to prove in a courtroom or a hearing. But from what I'm learning, a lot of people are afraid of Hirsch. As to whether his boys have ever roughed anybody up, we have no record of it."

"Thanks for the information," I told Lon.

"As long as the flow of information is a two-way street," he replied.

# CHAPTER 16

Wolfe sighed. "It is time for yet another meeting with Saul, Fred, and Orrie, who should have recovered from their Albany expedition," he said, omitting the words *you will arrange it for eleven o'clock tomorrow*. But then, I understood precisely what he meant without his having to be specific.

"I trust you all had a good night's sleep," Wolfe told the three in the office the next morning as they drank Fritz's coffee. "Travel, even short trips, can be enervating."

"I think we are all pretty well rested," replied Saul, probably the only one of the trio who knew the definition of enervating. "I think I can speak for all of us when I say that we are ready for whatever you have in mind."

"Excellent. Archie has been communicating with Lon Cohen, who was able to supply us with some information about

Miles Hirsch." Wolfe turned to me, and I gave them everything we had gotten from Lon about Hirsch.

"I'm surprised that I have never heard of him," Saul said. "He must keep a low profile."

"Cohen said Hirsch's clip file is very thin," I replied. "He probably likes it that way."

"I would like to shine some light upon this shadowy gentleman," Wolfe said. "Do you think you can learn more about his activities, nefarious or otherwise?"

"I don't just think so, I know so," Orrie added with his usual bravado. "Just turn us loose."

"I agree with Orrie," Saul said. "Having a place on Park Avenue means Hirsch must be spending a good chunk of his time in New York, which ought to help us. He's got to eat, so we should be able to find some of his hangouts. Also, it just happens that I'm in touch with a man up in Saratoga Springs who knows his way around their racetrack. He may be able to give us a steer regarding Hirsch's activities involving thoroughbreds."

"Saul, by all means, communicate with your Saratoga Springs man," Wolfe said. "To reiterate, we must cast a wide net to learn as much as possible about this individual, who spent time with Miss Carr in the Albany area. Are there any other suggestions?"

"As Saul says, the man has got to eat," Fred added. "We need to divide up the Midtown restaurants, particularly the more expensive ones, which are the places Hirsch is most likely to dine."

"And do we know his building on Park Avenue?" Orrie asked. "I can go over there and cozy up to the doorman."

Wolfe turned to me. "Archie, his address?"

I gave the number to Orrie, who jotted it down in his notebook and announced that co-op would be his first stop after our meeting broke up.

"I can start hitting the restaurants," Fred said. "Some of the maître d's have lockjaw when asked who their regulars are, but others like to brag about the famous people who are habitués."

"*Habitués*, eh? You've been working to improve your vocabulary. I am very impressed," said a smirking Orrie, who never misses a chance to needle Fred, perhaps in envy of the other man's plodding though tireless work ethic.

Durkin did not take the bait and just smiled tightly, while Saul played field general. "Okay, Mr. Wolfe, here is the plan: Orrie will start at that Park Avenue palace, while Fred and I will begin nosing around the swank eateries. We'll put together a list, and I'll take the ones east of Fifth Avenue in Midtown with Fred tackling the joints to the west. And, Orrie, when you're done on Park Avenue, you work the spots from Twenty-Third Street south."

If Cather did not like the assignment he was given, he remained mum, well aware that Panzer was a fair-haired boy in Wolfe's book, never mind that Saul's hair was as dark as a raven's feathers.

The meeting broke up, the boys headed out on their assignments, and Wolfe went to the kitchen to monitor Fritz's progress with lunch. If I were Fritz, I would banish Wolfe from his domain, but then, I am not owner of the brownstone and the employer of the best chef this side of Paris. And I really should not be too worried about Fritz Brenner, who has shown in the past that he can hold his own in any argument with his boss involving the use of such ingredients as tarragon, saffron, and sage.

Wolfe and I were in the office with coffee after lunch when the telephone rang—an excited Orrie Cather. "Archie, I've got a hot one," he said as I signaled Wolfe to pick up his receiver.

"I am on the line, Orrie. What have you learned?"

"After our meeting, Mr. Wolfe, I talked to the doorman at Hirsch's Park Avenue address and learned that he stays in New York about half the time, and that he likes Italian food. Then I started hitting the eateries in Little Italy. At the third restaurant I visited, La Trattoria Toscana, on Mulberry Street, which food lovers have told me is the best place in the neighborhood, I talked to the host, and bingo!"

"Go on, Orrie," Wolfe snapped.

"This guy is named Antonio, no surprise in a place like that. I slipped him a fin, which I figured might not be enough, but damned if it didn't set him to talking like a stool pigeon. Turns out that Miles Hirsch loves the joint and has dinner there at least once a week when he's in town, sometimes more often. He usually eats with two or more others, sometimes one of them a woman."

"Does he know when Mr. Hirsch will next visit the establishment?"

"No, but I've got that covered, Mr. Wolfe. I slipped good old Antonio another fin, and he said he will call me the next time Hirsch makes a reservation."

"And when that occurs, you will telephone us immediately," Wolfe said.

"Yes, sir, I will."

"Satisfactory, Orrie." After the call had ended, Wolfe turned to me. "Would it disconcert you to go to this restaurant and meet with Miles Hirsch?"

"I'm surprised you would ask. I don't get disconcerted easily."

"The man could very well be dangerous."

"So can I, under the right circumstances. I assume you want to see Hirsch."

"Your assumption is correct. Do you believe the act of bringing him here can be accomplished without violence?"

"I do. It is possible Orrie may call when you are upstairs with the orchids, or we are in the dining room."

Wolfe scowled. "We will deal with that contingency if it occurs."

We heard nothing from Orrie, Saul, or Fred the rest of the day, which meant the latter two had not discovered any restaurants patronized by Miles Hirsch. But we did have La Trattoria Toscana in our sights and had to hope we would get a call from Orrie Cather at some point.

That point came two days later, when Orrie phoned at two thirty and told me Hirsch had made a seven thirty reservation for that night.

After thanking Orrie and passing the information along to Wolfe, I told him I planned to be at the restaurant by eight o'clock.

"You will miss dinner."

"But you won't. If I can pry Hirsch loose, and that's a big 'if,' I may be able to get him here by the time you are finished with your veal birds in casserole and have returned to the office."

Wolfe made a face but said nothing and returned to his current book. He was grumpy because it was likely he would have to do some work tonight.

I managed to locate my favorite cabbie, Herb Aronson, who drove me to the restaurant on Mulberry Street. On our way down to Little Italy, I outlined the plan and told him I didn't know how long I would be inside.

"Don't worry, Archie. I'll keep the motor—and the meter—running. And per your orders, I will not attempt to engage your guest in conversation."

"Assuming I will be able to coax our guest to leave the restaurant and climb into your vehicle," I said. "See you in a while."

I went inside and saw a stout, dark-haired man in a tuxedo

at a podium just inside the dining room door. "Are you Antonio?" I asked.

"I am, sir," he said with the slightest of bows. "How may I assist you?"

"I have a message for Mr. Hirsch, and I understand that he is dining here tonight. Can you see that he gets this right now?"

Antonio knit his brow but nodded and took a folded sheet of paper from me on which I had printed, in block letters, two words. I watched as he strode across the half-filled dining room to a table in a back corner where three people sat—two men and a woman. The maître d' handed my note to the smaller of the men, a wiry fellow with a long face and white hair.

As I stood at the podium, Antonio gestured in my direction as the man who had the note peered at me, finally rising and walking in my direction. "What is the meaning of this?" he snarled, waving the sheet and looking up at me. He was probably five foot six.

"You are Miles Hirsch?"

"I am."

"Then the meaning should be obvious. My name is Archie Goodwin, and I work for the private investigator Nero Wolfe."

"Wolfe, huh? I've heard of him. Fat guy, isn't he? What do you—or he—want with me, for God's sake?"

"Mr. Wolfe would like you to visit him in his office and discuss the name on that piece of paper you're holding."

Hirsch continued glowering at me with icy blue eyes. "You can go straight to hell."

"That is where I may end up, all right. But for the present, I plan to go to the newspapers and tell them about a recent dinner you had at a roadhouse on Route 378 north of Albany." I turned on my heel and started to leave the Italian restaurant as Antonio looked on, wearing a puzzled expression.

"Wait a minute, Goodwin," Hirsch said. "Why does Wolfe want to see me?"

"There's one way to find out. Go to his residence. I have got a taxi running a tab right outside."

"Why doesn't he come here—or to my place on Park Avenue, if he wants to talk?"

"He does not leave home on business or for almost any other reason."

"Look, you've already interrupted my dinner, and that of my friends. I am not leaving here with you, so forget it, goddamn it!"

"Have it your way. But once you have finished what I'm sure is a fine meal, you're welcome to come to Mr. Wolfe's residence on Thirty-Fifth Street." I gave him the address.

He still was angry, but his glower had lost some of its intensity, probably because he was assessing his options. "All right, I will be there . . . later."

"We will be expecting you," I told him.

When I got back to the brownstone, Wolfe was in the office with beer, reading that week's *New York Times Magazine*. "I saw Mr. Hirsch in the restaurant and tried to get him to leave with me, but he wasn't having it. He says he will come to see us, but only after he finishes dinner."

"Do you believe him?"

"Let's put it this way: I have piqued his curiosity to the degree that I'm giving three-to-one odds he will show up."

"And just how did you pique the man's curiosity?"

I told Wolfe what I had printed on that sheet of paper that was handed to Hirsch. No sooner did I finish than the doorbell sounded.

Through the one-way glass, I could see a dour Hirsch and his male dinner companion, a beefy lug with a buzz cut who also wore a grim expression.

I went back to the office and said, "Hirsch brought a large friend, probably a bodyguard. Do I let him in?"

"Do you have Fred stashed in the front room again?" Wolfe was still slightly miffed about that little episode.

"Not tonight," I said.

"Do you think you are capable of handling the larger individual, should it become necessary?"

"Affirmative." I was a little riled myself, and I let Wolfe know it. As added protection, I had the Marley .38 in a shoulder holster hidden under my well-tailored suitcoat.

"Very well." He huffed out a breath. "Have them come in."

I swung open the front door. "Welcome, gentlemen. I will hang up your coats, and then it's down the hall to Mr. Wolfe's office." Hirsch let me take his coat, but his colleague did the job himself and then I led the way.

Wolfe looked up as we entered. "You are Mr. Hirsch," he stated, looking at the smaller man. "And your associate?"

"This is Harley Everts. He goes everywhere with me," Hirsch said, dropping into the red leather chair while Everts parked his bulk in one of the yellow ones.

"Will either of you like something to drink? I am having beer."

"We did not come here to drink," Hirsch snapped, settling into the chair that dwarfed him, "but . . . I will have a scotch and water. What about you?" he asked Everts.

"Sounds good," came the gruff reply. I mixed the drinks at the cart against the wall and passed them out.

"Okay, Wolfe, I have heard of you and know a little about your reputation, so I was curious when your man here invited me to see you," Hirsch said, taking a sip of scotch and nodding his approval. "Now just what's on your mind?"

"I would have thought that was obvious, given the note you received from Mr. Goodwin."

"You call that a *note*? It was just a name!"

"Indeed. And what does that name mean to you, Mr. Hirsch?"

"She is someone I happen to know, not that it is any of your business."

"You had a meal with Maureen Carr at a roadhouse north of Albany." Wolfe added the date and the approximate time.

"Who says so?" demanded Hirsch, folding his arms over his concave chest.

"Come, sir, this is an established fact. Do you deny its occurrence?"

"I do not have to admit or deny anything. I am not on trial."

"Not yet anyway. Are you aware Miss Carr has dropped out of sight, and that none of her friends have seen her in weeks?"

"Maybe that is by intent," Hirsch said.

"What did you discuss at your meal?"

"Again, I say, none of your business."

"A missing person report has been filed for Miss Carr," Wolfe improvised. "I am sure the authorities would be interested in learning that you may well be the only individual who has seen her in the last several weeks."

"Are you trying to blackmail me?" Hirsch said, lifting off the chair and leaning forward, jaw out.

"I do not indulge in blackmail, sir. But I am commissioned with learning the whereabouts of Miss Carr."

"Yeah, just who commissioned you?"

"That is irrelevant at present. Do you know where the lady is?"

"I do not."

"Have you seen her since your meeting in the Albany area?"

"No."

"I repeat my question: Do you know where she is?"

"Also, no, I haven't any idea."

"How do you happen to know Miss Carr, or do you claim that also is none of my business?"

"You have said it," Hirsch answered with a scowl.

"What about you, Mr. Everts?" Wolfe asked. "What role to you play in the affairs of Mr. Hirsch?"

The question took Everts by surprise, and he jerked upright. "I'm, I . . . help him wherever I can."

"Leave Harley out of this, Wolfe," Hirsch barked. "I find it helpful to have a protector, someone who can keep people from pestering me."

"Do you get pestered often?"

"I feel that I am being pestered right now!"

"I would hardly call my questions pestering. You split your time between residences in New York City and Saratoga Springs."

"That is no secret."

"I understand you are well known in the horse racing world."

"I have done all right at the tracks over the years," he replied, settling back and crossing one leg over the other.

"And you have your own stable of horses?"

"Say, you have done a lot of research on me, Wolfe. I suppose I should be flattered."

"Such was not my intent, sir. Jonathan Swift wrote that 'flattery's the food of fools,' and you are by no means a fool, so it would be futile to flatter you. Back to the horses, are you a gambler on the races?"

"I've been known to put a few dollars on certain ponies over the years."

"Would you say you have been successful?"

"Overall, I have done all right."

"Do you also loan funds to other gamblers?"

Hirsch stiffened. "I am really tired of answering your impertinent questions," Hirsch said, rising. As he stood, so did his silent partner, who glowered at me. I answered with a bland smile and walked the two of them down the hall in silence. I helped Hirsch with his coat but did not get thanks, not that I expected any.

The two men stepped into an idling blue Chrysler Imperial at the curb. My eyes are plenty good enough that as I stood on the stoop, I could read the numbers and letters on the New York plate as the car drove off.

# CHAPTER 17

"Well, that was one colossal waste of time," I said to Wolfe when I got back to the office after seeing Hirsch and his tight-lipped sidekick—or bodyguard—Everts out.

"I must disagree, Archie. Mr. Hirsch is now on his guard, which I had intended. He is aware that we have been delving into his activities, and his discomfort upon learning this tonight was manifest."

"I must have missed that discomfort."

"He was not the same man when he left as when he entered. He appears to be staying at his New York residence for the present, and I would like to ensure that he is under surveillance—and that he is aware of it."

"I gather you want tails put on him."

"I do. The cost is immaterial, as I will absorb that expense if Mr. Mason deems it to be exorbitant."

"Do you want Hirsch to be dogged around the clock?"

"Not quite. Let's leave the man alone between, say, two a.m. and eight a.m. Also, I don't want to use Saul, Fred, or Orrie on this project, as they may be needed elsewhere."

"We have not called on Del Bascom and his operation lately. Of course, his operatives can't hold a tail as well as Saul, but then, nobody can. They would still be my first choice."

"Mine as well," Wolfe agreed. "Telephone Mr. Bascom and discover what can be arranged. If he has men available, have them begin a surveillance of Mr. Hirsch's New York residence, noting when he leaves and returns. The surveillance need not be covert."

"Well, Archie Goodwin, of all people," Bascom answered his phone with a dry chuckle. "Haven't heard from you in ages. What's going on in the exciting world of Nero Wolfe Inc.?"

"You make it sound like we're some type of corporation, Del. But we are essentially a two-man operation, consisting of a CEO and an underappreciated wage slave."

"Poor fella, sorry I asked."

"How is business at your end?"

"Not bad, but it could always be better. I assume you've got a reason for calling."

"You assume right, as usual. Have you got any ops who are up for some tailing?"

"We have. Who do you want shadowed?"

"A nabob of sorts, name of Miles Hirsch, short, skinny, about five foot six, white hair."

"The name sounds vaguely familiar. Feed me a little more."

I gave Del a rundown on what we knew about Hirsch, including his Park Avenue address and the description of his bodyguard and his automobile, complete with the Chrysler's license number.

"Based on the times you want a man glued to Hirsch, I'd set up three six-hour shifts, complete with a taxi outside his building. It's gonna cost Wolfe. You want these to be covert tails?"

"No, we don't care if your men are spotted."

"And is this bodyguard of his armed?"

"Everts? I would bet on it."

"My men will be carrying pieces as well. But, Archie, I don't want to get them involved in this if there's going to be gunplay."

"I'm almost positive there won't be any of that. Hirsch likes to keep a low profile. Very little has been written about him over the years, and I am sure he wants to keep it that way."

"Okay, we've got a deal. When do we start?"

"Tomorrow morning."

"That's fine. There will be a man outside that Park Avenue building at eight o'clock. I suppose you want daily reports?"

"We do."

"I would have expected nothing less. You will hear from me every day, say around six. As I recall, that is when Wolfe comes down from playing with his posies, isn't it?"

"Yes, but he would hate to hear you call them posies."

"A rose by any other name," Del said, and we signed off.

The next evening's call came at 6:10 p.m., just after Wolfe had gotten settled in at his desk with beer and a new book, *Roosevelt and Hopkins*, by Robert E. Sherwood. I answered, was greeted with "Bascom reporting," and motioned Wolfe to pick up his phone.

"Here's today's report," Del said. "The Chrysler pulled up in front of the Park Avenue palace at nine fifteen a.m. and, with a chauffeur at the wheel, drove Hirsch and his ape to the Continental Bank branch on East Fifty-Fourth Street, with my man in a taxi trailing them at a discreet distance. Hirsch went into the bank alone and was there for twenty-two minutes. When he came out, he got back in the car, which then headed downtown to Eleventh Street near Sixth Avenue and stopped in front of a three-story brick building, the kind you see a lot of in the Village." Del gave its address.

"Both Hirsch and Everts went in, and they were there for thirteen minutes before leaving and getting back into the car, which then drove them back to Hirsch's Park Avenue digs."

"Two questions, Mr. Bascom," Wolfe said. "Did your man feel that he was spotted by Hirsch at any time? And did he—your man, that is—observe Hirsch and Everts enter Hirsch's Park Avenue building?"

"Yes, to both, Mr. Wolfe," Bascom said. "Because our assignment was specifically to keep an eye on Hirsch's activities and those of his henchman, my man made no effort to conceal himself, and he did see both men enter Hirsch's Park Avenue address. Do you want me to have someone keep a watch on the Eleventh Street home?"

"Not necessary. But continue to monitor Mr. Hirsch's activities until further notice."

"Let me guess our next move," I said to Wolfe after we ended the phone call. "We are going to have some combination of Saul, Fred, and Orrie stake out that four-story building in the Village."

"Perceptive, up to a point," Wolfe grunted. "We also need to learn the names of the domicile's residents, as well as the owner."

"I thought that went without saying." Another grunt as he went back to his book.

Knowing what was expected of me, I telephoned Saul Panzer and laid out the situation.

"I am familiar with the block, but not the specific building; I'll get on the case. Does Mr. Wolfe want it under surveillance?"

"He does indeed. Will you set that up?"

"Of course. In fact, I'll head over there right now to have a look."

Saul did not waste any time. He called back just before we were about to go into the dining room. "Thought you would be interested in this," he said. "I haven't gone into the place yet, but I have given it a look from the outside, and what do you know? It has a rear entrance that leads to a narrow walkway between buildings that puts you on Tenth Avenue. Remind you of anything?"

"Like a certain dwelling on West Thirty-Fifth Street?" I asked. "Makes it handy to leave the joint without being seen from the front."

"Much as you and Mr. Wolfe have been known to do on occasion—Fred, Orrie, and me, too, for that matter, especially when Inspector Cramer is pounding on the door. I am going to do some more poking around, and I will report with any progress."

Because Wolfe bans shoptalk during meals, I waited until we were in the office with coffee to give him an account of Saul's preliminary report on the Eleventh Street residence and its rear entrance.

"We tend to think it unique that we have what essentially is an escape hatch," Wolfe said, referring to the back way out of the brownstone, "although I suspect there are far more such exits in Manhattan than we realize, despite this island being devoid of alleys."

"I'll be more interested in what Panzer learns when he delves more deeply into the details of that place in the Village."

"Knowing Saul's tenacity and thoroughness, I am confident we will learn more in an expedient manner," Wolfe said.

I suppose 10:00 a.m. the next morning qualifies as expedient, because that was when we got another call from Saul.

"First, the house is a single-owner place, so there aren't any nameplates at the front entrance. Second, I got no answer when I rang the bell on several occasions last night and today. Third, I've got a friend at City Hall who I once did a favor for."

"Whoa, that is what Wolfe would call a non sequitur," I said. "Your third item has nothing to do with the first two."

"Okay, smart guy, so I may not have expressed myself well enough to suit someone who is getting much-needed lessons in English usage from Nero Wolfe. Through this individual I know at the hall, I was able to learn who owns the building. Her name is Elaine Musgrove, and I looked up her home address, which is—no surprise—that very building."

"And from what you have said, nobody's home."

"That appears to be the case," Saul said. "Shades, blinds, and curtains are all closed; the place looks like it's shuttered."

"Yet we know damn well that Hirsch and his lackey were just there and stayed for a few minutes."

"Which of course means we'll be keeping a watch on it—around the clock."

"You took the words right out of my mouth. We will remain in touch."

When Wolfe came down from the plant rooms at eleven and got himself settled with his beers and a book, I reported.

"Call Miss Rowan; I wish to speak to her," he ordered and opened the book to where he had bookmarked it.

"Good morning, lady of leisure," I said when she answered.

"Leisure, my foot," she shot back. "For the last two hours, I have been planning a May picnic with games and pony rides for a bunch of orphans up at my place in Katonah."

"I stand corrected and chagrined, well aware of the many good works you are involved with. Mr. Wolfe would like to take a few minutes of your valuable time." I stayed on the line as Wolfe picked up.

"Good morning, Miss Rowan. I am sorry to disturb you, but I have a question."

"Which I will try to answer."

"Good. Does the name Elaine Musgrove mean anything to you?"

There was a pause at the other end. "She . . . sounds familiar," Lily finally said. "A friend of Maureen's, maybe from college. Yes, that's it; I'm sure they were classmates."

"Indeed? Where did they attend university?"

"Radcliffe, which is part of Harvard. Now it's coming back to me. I have heard Maureen speak fondly of Elaine more than once, although I've never met her. The two of them are part of a group that has stayed very close since their university years. I always wished I'd had a similar bunch when I was at Barnard, but such was not the case. Do you think Elaine may know where Maureen is?"

"It is possible," Wolfe said.

"It also is possible that Eric Mason may know more about Elaine than I do. I'm sorry I can't be more helpful."

"You have been of more help than you realize, Miss Rowan," Wolfe said, hanging up as I stayed on the line. "It was a good suggestion of yours to call Mason," I told Lily.

"It's all I could think of right now. Please keep me apprised."

"Absolutely. After all, you *are* a client."

"Call Mr. Mason," Wolfe ordered after we signed off.

The advertising man picked up on the second ring, and when I identified myself, he muttered, "I wondered if I was ever going to hear from you and Wolfe again."

"We have been working. It's just that we haven't had anything significant to report. I've got a question: Do you know Elaine Musgrove?"

"Well, sort of. I have met her a couple of times, an old college chum of Maureen's. Seems like a nice gal. I think she has got a place down in the Village, although I have never been there."

"Does she go away in the winter months?"

"Yeah, to the French Riviera."

"Do you happen to know where she stays?"

"Oddly enough I do, because Maureen was there once years ago, and she mentioned what a great setup it was. Every winter Elaine spends at least a couple of months, maybe more, at a luxury villa on the grounds of a hotel in Cap d'Antibes."

"Do you know the name of the hotel?"

"Say, what's this all about?"

"We're not sure, but we think Elaine Musgrove might be able to help us locate Maureen, although I must tell you that it could be a long shot."

"At this point, I'll take that long shot," Mason said.

"It may mean sending one of our men to the Riviera."

"Fine by me. Just add whatever it costs to my bill, as long as your guy doesn't linger down there too long."

"He won't, he's all business. What's the name of the place where Elaine Musgrove is staying?"

"Oh yeah, it's the Hôtel de la Mer."

I thanked Mason, hung up, and swiveled to Wolfe for instructions.

# CHAPTER 18

When I had told Mason that the individual we'd send to the Riviera would be all business, I knew Wolfe was going to suggest Saul Panzer, and I was right. We both knew Saul never wasted time on a job, although he might appreciate the surroundings. We also realized that if we were to send Orrie Cather, there was the risk that he would find all manner of diversions on the beaches of the Mediterranean and would take his time returning to New York. I told our other client, Lily Rowan, that Saul was headed to France, and she approved.

Within hours and armed with instructions, Saul had booked himself on one of the newly launched overnight flights to Paris with a connecting plane to Nice. He seemed to approve of the assignment, but then, who wouldn't? A couple of days away from New York's early spring weather was always welcome.

But before leaving for Europe, Saul told Orrie he was in charge of keeping watch on the Greenwich Village building around the clock, which meant hiring one of Bascom's men to join Fred and Orrie on the twenty-four-hour surveillance.

"Think it's worth paying to have that place watched all the time?" I asked Wolfe. "There doesn't seem to be much going on inside."

"Normally, I would agree, although something in that building must have interested Mr. Hirsch and his dogsbody."

"I suppose. Maybe I'm worrying too much about expenses, but if Mason is willing to pony up to send Saul to France, what's a few bucks on a vigil?"

Just then, the phone squawked, and I started to answer with my usual "Nero Wolfe's office, Arch—" when I got a "Yeah, yeah, I know the spiel" from Lon Cohen at the *Gazette*.

"Something just came over the police wire that should interest you," he said. "A man identified as Everett Carr was found shot dead in a passageway between two buildings in Greenwich Village. If I remember right, and I usually do, you asked for the clips on that very same name sometime back."

I motioned and Wolfe picked up his receiver. "Any other details?" I asked.

"Carr had been hit, by somebody who pulled the trigger several times, because there were some shell casings on the ground from shots that missed him. He was identified by his wallet. That's all we have so far."

"Give me the address." Lon fed it to me and I thanked him, hanging up and turning to Wolfe. "I'm off," I said and received the slightest of nods in return.

I got lucky and found a taxi at the Ninth Avenue corner, told the cabbie to step on it, and was in the Village minutes later.

The address Lon gave was on Bank Street, not far from the place we were staking out. I left the taxi a half block from the flashing lights of two squad cars and an ambulance, with its crew in the process of hauling away a bag that certainly had a body inside. There was the usual gaggle of onlookers, along with several uniformed cops and a familiar figure, Sergeant Purley Stebbins of the New York Police Department's Homicide Squad. For me, a piece of bad luck.

As I approached, he recognized me and did not like what he saw. "Goodwin, I feel I am having a bad dream. What is it about corpses that attracts you?"

"I enjoy watching a pro in action, Purley. I just happened to be in the Village, and I was drawn to all these bright lights."

"You just 'happen to be' in all sorts of places," he snarled. Purley Stebbins has never liked me, and the feeling is mutual. But somehow, we have managed to coexist for years without doing violence to each other. Call it an uneasy truce.

"So what's happened here?" I asked, hoping I presented a picture of innocence.

Stebbins narrowed his eyes. "You really don't have any idea?"

I shrugged. "I was visiting a friend near here, and . . . well, you know how those things are."

"No, I don't know, Goodwin, and I don't give a good goddamn about your personal life," Stebbins growled. "I'm busy investigating a murder."

"Sorry, I won't get in the way. Who was the poor sap who just got hauled away?"

"Name's Carr. Now just beat it. You are not welcome here. Do I have to draw you a picture?"

"Not necessary, Purley," I said, walking away.

When I got back to the brownstone, Wolfe was at his desk, reading. He looked up when I entered the office, his eyebrows raised.

"I got to the place where Carr had been shot and was hoping I could talk to some young cop who would in all innocence answer questions. But that was not to be."

Wolfe, putting his book down, said, "Sergeant Stebbins."

"How could you possibly know that?"

"Inspector Cramer usually sends the sergeant out on the initial investigation of a murder. Consider your good fortune. It could have been worse. You might have run into that cretin Lieutenant Rowcliff."

"A good point. Anyway, I left, but it was too late. Now we both know damned well that Cramer will be coming to visit. It's not just a matter of if, but of when."

Wolfe's sour expression conceded my point, and he slammed his book shut, rising. "I believe we can expect Mr. Cramer tomorrow morning, probably shortly after eleven. Good night, Archie."

He had nailed it, all right. At 11:06 the next morning, as we both were in the office, Wolfe with beer and me with coffee, the doorbell rang.

"Admit him," Wolfe gruffed. "There is nothing to be gained by putting the man off, and we may learn something from his presence."

Through the one-way glass, I could see a blocky frame that could belong to only one person. I swung the door open and said, "Good morning, Inspector, it begins to look like spring is really on the way."

His answer sounded something like "Grr" as he pushed by me and barreled down the hall to the office, his overcoat flapping like the wings of an overweight goose taking off.

By the time I got there, Cramer already had lowered himself into the red leather chair he had occupied more times than any other visitor to the brownstone.

Wolfe considered him. "I haven't seen you for some time, Mr. Cramer. I hope you have been well."

"I've been fine, mainly because I haven't had occasion to come here lately," the inspector said, jamming an unlit cigar into his mouth. "But, as they say, all good things must come to an end."

"A pessimistic view of life, sir," Wolfe remarked.

"That's what my job has done to me."

"Not surprising. You see the worst of the human species, and on a daily basis. You have my sympathy."

"I don't need your sympathy, Wolfe. What I need is to know why this man"—he gestured at me with his unlit cigar— "happened to be on a street in Greenwich Village so soon after someone was found shot dead there."

Wolfe turned to me. "Archie?"

That was my cue to show some of our cards to the inspector. "We have been interested in Everett Carr for some time."

"Interested—why is that?"

"His sister, Maureen, disappeared, and Mr. Wolfe has been hired to find her. Everett was her only living relative, and he, too, recently had been out of sight as well."

"Is this true?" Cramer barked, turning to Wolfe.

"Yes. Why would you doubt Mr. Goodwin?"

"Oh, now that's a question I could have fun with. He's more slippery than a greased pig and has been as long as I've known him. By the way, I'm guessing—and it is an educated guess— that your old pal Cohen at the *Gazette* tipped you off about Carr's shooting."

"Does it matter how Archie learned of the event?" Wolfe asked.

"I suppose not," Cramer conceded. "What do you know about Everett Carr?"

Wolfe looked in my direction. Another cue for me to open up.

"Everett came from a lot of money, like his sister. But unlike her, he was not the least bit careful with it. He had a gambling addiction from what we've learned and spent big bucks on the horses without much success. The last we knew, he had been living at that big YMCA on Thirty-Fourth Street, but he apparently hadn't been there the last few weeks."

"What about his sister?" Cramer asked.

"Maureen Carr has been a will-o'-the-wisp," Wolfe said.

"Which is your fancy way of saying you have failed in your search for her, is that right?"

"Thus far, you are correct, Inspector."

"Well, this is a side of you I don't often see, Wolfe. The great detective flummoxed, to use his own word."

"I prefer 'temporarily stalemated.' As you can see, Mr. Goodwin and I have been forthcoming and open. What can you tell us about the death of Mr. Carr?"

"Not a lot, yet. One item you might find interesting, though. Whoever got him must have been really sore at the victim, because several shots were fired, one of which apparently got him in the pump, but a few others missed completely. On the ground, our men found shell casings, and they were nine millimeter."

"That's a little unusual," I put in.

"Yes and no," Cramer said. "They used to be more unusual here, but since the war ended, we have begun to see them involved in shootings."

"That's the ammo Lugers use."

"Exactly, Goodwin!" Cramer rasped. "GIs have been bringing these German pistols home as souvenirs, I am sorry to say. They have been used in a number of murders, and, maybe saddest of all, in suicides as well."

"You are of course referring to the alarming number of

returning servicemen who have taken their own lives," Wolfe said.

"I am. Our soldiers, sailors, marines, airmen, they have accomplished great things overseas, and they have been praised and honored by the foreign countries they have defended, but it seems some of them haven't found life back home nearly as welcoming."

"We appreciate our troops during war, but we, too, often forget our debt to them soon after the guns have been silenced," Wolfe said.

"Very true," Cramer replied. "Whose quote is that?"

"Mine. Have you learned anything about Mr. Carr and how he happened to be in Greenwich Village?"

"No. I've gone over what was found on his person, and it is not very revealing. His clothes were shabby, and his driver's license listed that YMCA you mentioned as his address. According to the license, he was fifty-five, meaning he would have been too old to serve during the war. This doesn't look like a robbery. In his pocket was a money clip with thirty-four dollars in it, and his wristwatch was a cheapie, the kind you can buy at Woolworth's. He also carried two keys, one of them probably to his room at the Y, and there was a pack of Lucky Strikes with a couple of smokes left in it.

"Besides the driver's license," Cramer continued, "his wallet contained a picture of a somewhat young woman, perhaps a girlfriend or his sister, a couple of horse racing tickets—obviously for horses that had finished out of the money—and three addresses with phone numbers, very possibly of bookies, scribbled on a sheet of paper. We plan to call these numbers to see if whoever answers can tell us anything about Carr."

"How did you find out about the shooting?" I asked.

"A woman living on the block said she faintly heard a shot

and called the local precinct. Turns out the murder took place in a narrow passage between two buildings, which may have muffled the noise to some degree. Whoever plugged Carr was facing him, up close in that tight space, suggesting that he may have known his killer."

"Is violence common in the neighborhood?" Wolfe asked.

"Not really. I can't remember the last time there was a murder within blocks of what happened," Cramer said as he rose to leave. "You will let me know if and when you locate the dead man's sister, won't you?"

The inspector got no reply from Wolfe as he walked out of the office and down the hall to the front door, which I locked behind him. "At least he didn't throw his cigar at the wastebasket this time," I said to Wolfe, who shook his head in disgust and returned to reading his book.

# CHAPTER 19

The early edition of the *Gazette*, an evening paper, usually hits our front stoop a little after noon, and this day was no exception. I brought it in and found the item, headlined "Man Shot Dead in the Village," on page four. The five-paragraph piece added nothing to what we already knew. I handed the paper to Wolfe, who read the item and made a face. "We will be hearing from our clients, of course," he said.

"Assuming they get this edition, or if there has been something about the killing on the radio, which is a strong possibility, and—" I was interrupted by the phone.

"Goodwin, I just learned about Maureen's brother," Eric Mason said sharply. "What do you know about it?"

"Probably not much more than you do," I replied, neglecting to tell him I had been on the scene.

"I want to know what you and Wolfe are going to do about this. And more important, have you gotten anywhere on finding Maureen? I have this feeling that nothing is going on."

I cupped my mouthpiece and whispered to Wolfe, "Mason's on the line, and he's hot. Want to talk to him?"

"Hello, Mr. Mason, this is Nero Wolfe."

"I just told Goodwin that it seems like you have gotten nowhere in finding Maureen. And now, with her brother dead, the situation is worse, it's dire. Good God, she may not even be alive, for all we know."

"We have no reason whatever to believe Miss Carr is deceased," Wolfe said. "And we continue to explore new avenues in locating her."

"You sound like you are stringing me along."

"I am sorry you feel that way, sir. If you prefer, we can negate our relationship, which would free you to find other means of attempting to locate the woman."

There was no response on the line for what seemed like a minute but was less than half that. The silence was broken by a loud exhale, and then, "No . . . sorry, my nerves were already frayed, and now, with what happened in the Village last night . . . no, go on with your work." Mason hung up without waiting for a response.

"I had better call Lily and bring her up to date," I told Wolfe, who nodded his approval.

"I hope I'm not disturbing something important," I said after she picked up.

"Not at all, my dear. As you are all too aware, I tend to start my day slowly. I am just now finishing breakfast—a very hearty and delicious breakfast, although probably not of the same quality as you receive each morning from Fritz."

"Still, I do not think you're being deprived. I would like to start your day—even though it is after noon—on a positive note, but I have some disturbing news: Maureen's brother, Everett, was shot dead last night in Greenwich Village."

"Oh, Archie. What . . . happened. Who . . . who did it?"

"Sorry to say we don't have any answers yet, nor do the police. There apparently were no eyewitnesses. And before you ask, we still don't have any leads regarding Maureen."

"I should call Sofia. I haven't talked to her for a few days, and I'm sure that if she had heard anything, she would have let me know."

"Good idea to check in with her," I said. "Let us know what, if anything, you are able to learn."

We heard from Saul Panzer two days later. He called and identified himself as I was in the office after breakfast. "This sounds like a local call, which means you are not sunning yourself on some Riviera beach that looks like a travel agency poster advertising France."

"No such luck, although it was tempting to stay at least another day," Saul said. "The hotel was top-notch, and the service was something I could easily get used to. I can stop by and report when Mr. Wolfe comes down from the roof, assuming there are no objections."

None whatever, I told him. And sure enough, he already was settled in the red leather chair with coffee when Wolfe strode into the office at just after eleven, settled into his reinforced chair, and rang for beer. "I trust your flights were without incident," he asked Saul.

"Everything went smoothly, thanks. And as I told Archie, the living is good down there in the South of France. But then, you don't want to hear me spout a travelogue."

"Perhaps not, but I am comforted to learn that this assignment did not prove to be a trial. Before we continue, are you aware that Everett Carr was shot dead in Greenwich Village three nights ago?"

Saul took in air and shook his head. "No, what are the details?"

"We will supply them later. What did you learn on your trip?"

"First, that Elaine Musgrove is a peach, and I don't toss that word around recklessly. She welcomed me to her villa as if I were an old friend. When I told her the current situation, she was genuinely concerned about her classmate," Saul said, consulting his notebook. "'Just after I had left New York and got down here for a two-month stay,' she said, 'Maureen cabled and asked me if she could stay at my house in the Village for a while.'

"'I was puzzled by her request, since her own place on Park Avenue is every bit as nice as what I've got downtown. But she seemed agitated over the telephone, which is unlike her, and it was quickly clear to me she did not want to talk about whatever her problem is. I knew she wouldn't make a request like this without a very good reason, so I told the caretaker to make sure that she got a key.'

"We talked a lot more and even had dinner together one night," Saul said, "and it was easy to see how close these two have been, going way back to their college years. Miss Musgrove said she had no idea what might have driven her longtime friend to go into hiding. At that point, I asked about the brother and she looked uncomfortable.

"'Maureen almost never talks about him,' she said. 'It's not as though she's ashamed of him, exactly, more like she's disappointed. Everett never married, not that it's such a bad thing, but he doesn't seem to need or want companionship of any kind. His behavior makes him the classic example of a loner.'

"I asked if he is an alcoholic," Saul continued, "and she said that seems likely. But she added that given what she had learned from Maureen, he had a serious addiction, not to drugs but to gambling, particularly horse racing, which is no surprise to us, of course."

"Did Miss Musgrove say she had met Everett Carr?" Wolfe asked.

"She had, but only on a few occasions. To her, he seemed withdrawn, sullen, possibly suffering from some sort of depression, and he obviously was not interested in his appearance. 'Seeing him, it was hard to believe that he had come from a wealthy family,' she said, adding that his sister had a pained look when she was with him."

"I should think so," I said. "It's hard to see someone going down the drain before your eyes."

"Well, from what you have told me, he is all the way down that drain now," Saul observed. "Give me the details."

We filled him in on the Greenwich Village shooting and on Cramer's visit to the brownstone. "Maybe Everett's death will flush his sister out from her hideaway, or is that wishful thinking?"

"No, I do not believe it is," Wolfe said. "Word will by some channel reach Miss Carr about her brother's death, if it has not already, and she will emerge from what may be a self-imposed exile."

"Good point," Saul said. "By the way, I should have mentioned this sooner—Elaine Musgrove gave me a key to her house."

. I started to bark *Yes, damn it, you really should have mentioned it sooner!* but before I could spit the words out, Wolfe said, "I was hoping to hear that, Saul. A visit to that residence is in order."

"You heard the man, Archie. Let's go."

"Saul, I must intercede here," Wolfe said. "There will be plenty of time to make that trip to Greenwich Village after lunch. Today's carte is broiled shad with sorrel sauce and Fritz's special bread. There will be enough for three."

"Now *you* heard the man, Mr. Panzer," I said. "I vote with my employer."

"I gracefully yield to the majority," Saul said with a salute, and we went to the dining room.

It was after two thirty when we climbed out of a cab at Elaine Musgrove's home on Eleventh Street. "Looks quiet," I remarked and Saul nodded. He pulled out the key he had gotten in France and opened the front door. We tiptoed in, guns drawn, as if we were expecting company, but we were met only with silence.

By preagreement, I took the ground floor while Saul went upstairs to do his prowling. From everything I saw, the place appeared to be immaculate. Living room, formal dining room, den, and kitchen all were for company. Not even a layer of dust, which would have been expected in the time the lady of the house had been absent.

I went one up one flight and found Saul in what looked like a sitting room, opening drawers and turning over cushions. "Did Miss Musgrove ever tell you that she had a cleaning woman?"

"I asked, and she said, 'Why should I bother? Each time I come back from France or elsewhere, I have someone come in and do a thorough dusting and sweeping, and she then comes every week after that. Why should I bother keeping the house in pristine condition when I am away? After all, who is here to appreciate it?'"

"The lady has a solid argument," I told Saul. "But that being the case, why do things seem so spotless here now?"

"Archie, I have been asking myself that for the last few minutes. So far, I haven't seen any signs of dust."

"Which means someone—presumably Maureen Carr—has been here recently, very recently."

"And yet, when I went through the bedrooms, everything was neat and tidy," Saul said. "I couldn't see any sign of recent habitation—except . . ."

"Habitation, now there's a word Nero Wolfe would use. Wait—what do you mean, *except*?"

"No matter how well a place gets swept and cleaned up, one thing that is damned near impossible to get rid of is cigarette smoke, and it was definitely in the air in one of the guest bedrooms."

"So maybe Maureen is a smoker," I said, "although in the few times I have seen her, I don't recall seeing her with a cigarette."

"What about her late brother?" Saul asked.

"Yes, of course!" I said, slapping my forehead. "When Carr's body was searched, the cops found an opened package of cigarettes, Luckies."

"Which makes it highly possible that both sister and brother had been camping out in the Musgrove residence."

"And before they made their exit—maybe because Hirsch and his thug had paid them a visit—Maureen must have done some fast tidying up." Saul and I continued going through the house from top to bottom without turning up anything significant, although for the record, I also smelled cigarette smoke in one of the rooms.

"Sorry to say this, Archie, but I don't think that we are any closer to finding Maureen Carr than we were before."

"Maybe not, although it's just possible that she has returned to her Park Avenue digs."

Saul lifted a shoulder. "Hey, it's worth a visit, at least to see the guy who works in front, the one you said you've met."

We hailed a taxi, whose driver seemed to be in training for the Indianapolis 500 auto race. I shouldn't complain, though, because he never hit a car, a bus, or another cab, although at least part of the reason for that good fortune was the skill and the honking of the other drivers on the streets he raced along, changing lanes as if he were indeed on that storied Indiana "brickyard."

When, with a screech of brakes, we pulled up in front of Maureen Carr's building, I paid the hackie. I was pleased to see Seamus, the doorman, standing erect at his post out front. "You may not remember me," I told him as the taxi roared away.

"Ah, but I do," he said with a pleasant Irish lilt and a tip of his billed cap. "I have been told that I have a good eye for faces, and a good memory as well. You would be Mr. Goodwin, if I am not mistaken, and you were here not so very long ago with Sofia and Miss Rowan."

"You are correct. This is my very good friend Mr. Panzer, and we are here to ask if you have seen Miss Carr since the last time I came."

"Ah, I of course know Mr. Panzer and have for years, I am happy to say. As for Miss Carr, I have not encountered the lady now for several weeks. I do hope her absence from here is not a cause for concern. She has been away before, of course, but usually not for this long a period."

"Has Sofia come during that time, other than when we were here along with Miss Rowan?"

"Yes, once, and Miss Rowan also came again, to pick up mail on two occasions. I hope I was not overstepping my authority by allowing her to go upstairs. She showed me a key."

"Oh no, not in the least," I assured him and thanked him. He then flagged us a cab, and as we pulled away, I looked out of the back window, seeing the concern etched on his usually smiling face.

# CHAPTER 20

After dropping Saul off at his apartment on Thirty-Eighth Street, I got home to find that Fritz had left a note on my desk informing me that Lily had called.

"Goodwin reporting," I said when she answered.

"I talked to Sofia a little while ago to see how she was," Lily said in a subdued tone, "and she was extremely upset."

"Uh-oh. Has she heard from Maureen?"

"If she has, she didn't say so. No, it is more that she is worried about her husband and his . . . troubles."

"What kind of troubles?"

"It seems that Stan has been gambling away his paychecks on the horses."

"Shades of the late Everett Carr."

"That occurred to me, too," Lily said. "It's possible they may have known each other, although I doubt that they met through

Maureen, given that she and her brother have seen so little of each other in recent years."

"I don't know a lot about the world of horseplayers, but it's possible they tend to gravitate toward one another, trading information. And someone, I can't remember who, told me once that the bookies like to introduce gamblers to one another because it increases their own traffic. Did Sofia say what she plans to do about her husband's problem?"

"No, but right now she is far more concerned about Stan Jurek's addiction than about Maureen. I think she's particularly worried about their financial condition. She says her husband is frittering away money. And right now, she is not contributing because she hasn't had any income from Maureen for several weeks."

"Yeah, a tough situation. Has she even talked to him about it?"

"Yes, and according to her, he doesn't see that he has a problem, and he gets angry whenever she raises the subject."

"Alcoholics, gamblers, they don't always recognize or admit reality. I am sorry to hear about this, but it doesn't help us any in our hunt for Maureen Carr."

"I know, and I wish I had an idea that might aid us. Did Saul get any inkling from Elaine Musgrove as to why Maureen might have wanted to leave her Park Avenue place and go to Greenwich Village?"

"He did not, although he of course asked, hoping their longtime friendship might have made Miss Musgrove a close confidante of Maureen's."

"What do you plan to do now?" Lily asked.

"What I always do when I'm stumped: push Wolfe to figure things out."

"Over the long haul, that has seemed to work out quite well, wouldn't you say?"

"It has, but sometimes the challenge is to keep him focused.

As I have told you before, he's been known to run off the rails on occasion and go on an eating binge in frustration."

"Well, I wish you luck. I don't envy you."

"I don't envy me, either, at least as far as this particular situation is concerned. However, I *do* envy myself regarding the upcoming evening, when I will be dancing with an adorable partner at the Churchill."

"Anybody ever tell you what a good fellow you are? See you later," Lily said, and before I responded, the line went dead.

No more than five minutes later, Wolfe's elevator brought him down from the plant rooms, and he settled in at his desk. Just after he had rung for beer, I gave him a verbatim report on my conversation with Lily.

After I finished, he sat, eyes closed and arms folded. There was a chance he would begin that lip exercise that invariably leads to a solution, or that he would go into one of his funks. Neither occurred.

"Archie, get Saul, Fred, and Orrie. I want them here at nine p.m. tonight."

"Any special instructions?"

"No, I will give them instructions when they arrive."

"Because this is getting to be such a regular thing, maybe I should set up a schedule in which all three of them would come to the brownstone at the same time every day. I think that would—"

"Archie, shut up!"

"Yes, sir," I said as I turned to my telephone and Wolfe picked up his current book. By the time we went into the dining room for dinner, I had gotten okays from Fred and Orrie for nine and had left a message with Panzer's answering service.

Just after we finished eating and returned to the office, Saul called and said he could make it at nine but was puzzled as to what the meeting was for. "Sorry," I told him, "I am only the errand boy here. Be patient; you will have to wait to get your curiosity satisfied."

The trio were prompt as always, with Saul seated in the red leather chair and Fred and Orrie parked in the yellow ones as Wolfe considered them. "Archie suggests, facetiously, that because these conferences have become increasingly frequent, we should make them part of an ongoing schedule. However, as pleased as I am to see you all here, I also realize that because you are independent operatives and have other projects, I only have a limited claim upon your time."

"Understood, Mr. Wolfe," Saul said. "But I believe I can speak for Fred and Orrie in saying we all try to be available when you need us."

"Satisfactory. Now to a project that may take a good deal of your time in upcoming days. I would again like to have around-the-clock surveillance, but this time of a different residence. Archie, what is the address of the apartment building in Morningside Heights where Sofia Jurek and her husband reside?"

I tried to not show my surprise as I gave him the street number. "It's a four-story brick walk-up in a block full of similar structures and is in the second block west of Broadway. For the record, the Jureks live on the third floor, unit 317."

"Who are we supposed to be watching?" Saul asked. "There must be at least a couple of dozen tenants in the building."

"I am interested in the activities of both of the Jureks—his name is Stanley," Wolfe said. "And I realize none of you has seen them, so Archie can supply descriptions."

"Excuse me, Mr. Wolfe," Fred said, tentative as always in my boss's presence. "I also have seen Mr. Jurek."

"Of course, my apologies," Wolfe said, the corner of his mouth twitching in his version of a smile. "Not only has Mr. Durkin seen the man, he has taught him an excellent, if somewhat violent, lesson in manners, which Archie and I appreciated. You must tell your colleagues about it sometime, Fred. Describe Mr. Jurek to them."

Durkin cleared his throat. "This Jurek is a big guy, stocky with a beer gut, about six feet, light brown hair, crew cut, square face. That sound about right to you, Archie?" I said I agreed and added that he walks with a swagger.

"Okay, but what about the wife, what's her name, Sofia?" Orrie asked.

"She's petite, maybe one hundred ten pounds, no more than five foot two, short dark hair, almost black, a turned-up nose, and dark eyes, set close together," I said. "Also, she is somewhat hunched over, which seems odd for someone in her twenties, but then, she's been through a lot. Displaced from her home in Poland during the war, she was taken in by the British, where she met her GI husband. She seems meek, but some of that may be because that husband of hers is the domineering and over-protective type."

"All right, that's a start," Orrie said. "But what is it that we're looking for? Do we follow them when they leave the building? The man goes to work every day, in Brooklyn, isn't that right?"

"Let him go off to work, Orrie. I am more interested in the woman right now," Wolfe said, "and who, if anyone, she is with when she emerges from the building."

"Who would she be with?" Saul posed. "They have no children."

"This may well amount to nothing," Wolfe conceded, "but I would like to keep watch on the address, perhaps for several days. Do any of you feel this to be an imposition?"

Three men shook their heads, almost in unison. As is the case with most private ops, money is always welcome.

Saul said, "I will arrange the schedule, and"—he looked at Fred and Orrie—"before either of you start to complain, we will rotate in taking the graveyard shift, starting with me tonight. Any other instructions, Mr. Wolfe?"

"Report to Archie daily, or more often if events warrant it. And do not allow yourselves to be seen."

Wolfe really was chasing rainbows this time, but I wasn't about to tell him so, because he would have said to me, as he has in the past, *Do you have a better idea?*

I didn't, and as I saw the boys out of the brownstone, they looked as puzzled by this assignment as I was—even Saul, who rarely is puzzled about anything.

# CHAPTER 21

Starting the next morning, Saul telephoned me just after nine to report on the previous day's findings. For each of the first two days of surveillance, Stan Jurek left home at 6:16 a.m. and walked east to Broadway, where he entered a subway station, presumably to take the long ride to his job in Brooklyn, and each evening he returned home by 5:20. On the second day, he was toting a six-pack of beer.

Sofia left home both days as well. On day one, she emerged onto the street at 11:12 in the morning and walked to the grocery store down the block, stayed inside for twenty-three minutes, then walked back home carrying a bag of groceries that included a loaf of bread sticking out of the top. On the second day, she came out just after eleven and went to the drugstore at the Broadway corner, returning ten minutes later carrying a small sack.

I thanked Saul and wondered if the surveillance may well amount to nothing, to use Wolfe's own words. Assuming we were charging Eric Mason for the day rates of three veteran detectives, his eventual bill figured to be a corker.

On the morning of the next daily report, I felt it was time to tell Wolfe the surveillance was a wasted effort and that we should cut our losses. But that all changed when Saul telephoned.

"I was on the morning shift yesterday," he said, "and as you will recall, the rain was coming down hard. At just after ten, Sofia came out of her building in a raincoat and with an umbrella, and she was not alone."

"Go on," I said, tightening my grip on the receiver.

"The other individual, a couple of inches taller than Sofia, also wore a raincoat, which had a hood. The two of them were huddled together under the umbrella so closely that I couldn't see the face of the second person, but it had to be a woman."

"Why, Saul?"

"The shoes. They were definitely a women's style, with about two-inch heels."

"Where did they go?"

I heard a sigh. "What I am going to tell you does not reflect well upon me, Archie, and I won't charge for my time today—that would be like stealing from Mr. Wolfe."

"We will leave it to him to decide that. Now tell me what happened, no matter how much it pains you to unburden yourself."

"The pair walked east to Broadway in the rain, which had intensified. They got lucky and hailed a southbound Yellow cab right away, but when I got to the corner only seconds later, there wasn't a damned taxi in sight. Plain and simple, I had lost them."

"But they came back, right?"

"Wrong. That is, Sofia came back at about three alone and went into the building. I would love to ask where she had been and who she was with, but our instructions were to not identify ourselves."

"You not being able to grab a cab was a bad break," I sympathized.

"Well, I may be able to salvage a little pride, but it's a long shot."

"Out with it, man!"

"If nothing else, I got the taxi's number as it pulled away. I passed it along to a guy I did a favor for once who works in the Hack Bureau, the agency that licenses the city's cabs. I haven't heard back from him, and even if I do, he may not want to tell him who owns the Yellow."

"How big was the favor you did for him?"

"Big enough that it probably kept him out of the hoosegow."

"That would seem to give you some leverage."

"We'll see," Saul said, sounding less than optimistic.

When Wolfe came down from the plant rooms, I filled him in on Panzer's report.

"Saul has no reason whatever to chastise himself," Wolfe said. "I am assured that he will wring some information out of his source in that licensing agency." My boss's faith in Saul Panzer's abilities was unlimited, and my own confidence in him was much the same.

Our faith was merited when I answered the telephone that afternoon, just after Wolfe had gone up to play with the orchids. "I got the cabbie," Saul said.

"Wonderful. Can you bring him here?"

"I can, say at six, when Mr. W. comes down from the plant rooms. I'll pay him myself for his time."

"Six works. And as for any payment to the hack driver, we will discuss it."

I then called Wolfe on the house phone. "Yes!" he barked in his usual telephone tone.

"I know you hate to be disturbed when you're up in the greenhouse, but I did not want you to be surprised when you came down to the office. Saul has located the cabdriver who picked up Sofia and her companion. They will be here at six."

"Satisfactory," Wolfe said, hanging up. That was the first time he had ever used that word of praise after being interrupted during one of his sessions with the orchids.

The doorbell rang at 5:58 p.m., and when I opened the front door, Saul was there with a short, swarthy man sporting a black mustache, a flat cap, and a black leather jacket.

"Archie, this is Max Jacobs. Max, Archie Goodwin is an assistant to Nero Wolfe, whose house this is." I shook hands with Jacobs, and we walked down the hall just as Wolfe was emerging from the elevator.

Once we all were seated in the office, with Jacobs in the red leather chair, Saul did the introductions. "Would you like something to drink, sir?" Wolfe asked. "I am having beer."

"Uh, thanks a lot, beer is good for me, too."

Before Wolfe could hit the buzzer to call Fritz, Saul stood and said, "I'll get the beers. Milk for you, Archie?"

By the time Saul returned from the kitchen with a tray of drinks and frosted steins, Wolfe was asking Jacobs how he liked being a taxi driver.

"It's okay, although, lately, it seems like the tips are pretty skimpy. I can't say exactly why."

"I am sorry to hear that. We are still recovering from the war and all the shortages it has justifiably caused, and perhaps people are still cautious in their spending, which would seem to be understandable."

"Yeah, I'm sure you're right," Jacobs said, nodding and taking a sip of his beer. "But I can live with that. We all should. I served myself, in the Italian campaign, and after seeing what those poor people over there had to go through, I'm just glad we've done everything here to win the damned war, even if it means going without some stuff."

"Admirably stated," Wolfe said. "Mr. Panzer tells me you have some information for us."

"Before we go on," Saul said, "Max stepped forward, willing to help. We came here in his cab, which is at the curb with its meter running. I don't want him to lose revenue, and I will pay his fare."

"Mr. Jacobs will receive his fare—and more. Now, sir, I realize Mr. Panzer already has asked you some questions regarding a trip you made from Morningside Heights. Can you tell Mr. Goodwin and me about it?"

"Sure. The rain was comin' down pretty hard as I headed south on Broadway, and these two people, turned out they were both women, jumped off the curb and flagged me down. I damn near hit one of them. Anyway, they hopped in and told me to go to a bank at Forty-Third and Madison—it's a branch of Continental."

"How would you describe your passengers?" Wolfe asked.

"They both were young and, I don't know, I guess nervous, or maybe just cold from the rain. The temperature was just above freezing. They were shaking, and they said no more than a few words during the trip, and those I could barely hear."

"When you let them off at the bank, did they ask you to wait?"

"Nope, they seemed to be in a hurry. The taller one acted like she was in charge. I waited to watch them go inside, and then I pulled away."

"I hope they paid you."

"Oh yeah, the shorter one did, although there was no tip. But as I told you before, I'm plenty used to that. It's just the way things are."

"Thank you very much, sir," Wolfe said. "Archie, will you get one hundred dollars from the safe and give it to Mr. Jacobs?"

Saul started to protest, but I waved it aside and got the money out in twenties, handing it to Jacobs, who looked as if he had just won the Irish Sweepstakes. He was still expressing his thanks to Wolfe as Saul led him out.

"Well," I said after they had gone, "I believe that I know what comes next."

"Which is?"

"Yet another call to our friend Mortimer M. Hotchkiss, at the Continental Bank and Trust Co."

"It is comforting to know that I am predictable, Archie. We will place a telephone call to him tomorrow morning."

# CHAPTER 22

At just after eleven the next morning, Wolfe, fresh from his playtime with the orchids, settled in at his desk, inquired as to whether I had slept well, and rang for beer. After watching the foam settle in the stein and taking a sip, he turned to me, nodding. That was his way of indicating that I should now call Mortimer Hotchkiss of the Continental Bank & Trust Co.

I knew the bank's number by heart, and after a few rings, I got a functionary. He passed me along to another male individual, who acted like he had some standing in the bank's hierarchy. "May I ask who wishes to speak with Mr. Hotchkiss?"

"Nero Wolfe," I said. After a pause, the voice said, "Hold the line, please."

When the vice president came on, I nodded to Wolfe, who said, "Good day, Mr. Hotchkiss."

"Good day to you as well, Mr. Wolfe. How may I be of help?"

"You will recall our recent conversation. I am in need of further information concerning the subject of that talk."

That brought a long pause, after which Hotchkiss replied cautiously, "Please tell me what it is that you need, Mr. Wolfe."

"I request confirmation that another large withdrawal has been made from the account of the subject, and I make this request with great respect for you, sir. I would not be asking for this information were it not because of the danger I feel said subject could be in."

"May I call you back in just a few minutes?"

Wolfe said yes and gave Hotchkiss our number. Seven minutes later, the phone rang and we both picked up.

"Mr. Wolfe," Hotchkiss said, "in regards to our talk a few minutes ago, I can give you the confirmation you desire."

"I will ask for nothing more than that, sir," Wolfe said. "You have my thanks and my admiration for your principles and your dedication to duty."

"So we know that Maureen Carr has coughed up some more dough," I told Wolfe after he and the banker had ended their call. "Where do we proceed from here?

"We know from Saul that Sofia Jurek returned home from that trip to the bank, but she was alone. Which raises two questions: Where did the elusive Maureen Carr go, assuming that was her with Miss Jurek? And should we still keep watch on the Jureks' building?"

"The second question first," Wolfe replied. "We will drop the surveillance immediately. As to Miss Carr's destination after that trip to the bank, I am interested in your thoughts."

That is Wolfe's way of saying it seems like he might be stumped, although I haven't seen him stumped very often.

"All right," I said, "I will tell you where I think she did *not* go. One, Elaine Musgrove's Greenwich Village home. Reason:

Hirsch already knew she had been staying there. Two, her own place on Park Avenue. Reason: Hirsch knew her address. And the last person she wanted to run into was Miles Hirsch."

Wolfe closed his eyes and steepled his fingers. "Which of course leaves—"

"Damn it, of course it does!" I shouted, bolting from my chair, dashing down the hall, and grabbing my coat and hat without breaking stride as I headed for the front door.

I climbed out of a taxi at my destination. The doorman smiled and nodded at me as I entered the lobby and made for the automatic elevator. After all, he had seen me often enough, and he knew exactly where I was going. No name was needed. Getting out of what the British call the "lift," I crossed the hall to the door and rang the bell. The door immediately swung open, telling me that the doorman had called upstairs, announcing my arrival.

"Somehow, I expected to see you," Lily Rowan said, looking up at me with an expression that seemed to be half relief and half concern.

"How long has she been here?" I asked.

"Since late this morning. Need I tell you that Maureen is a nervous wreck?"

"I'm hardly surprised to hear that. But at least she has been found. What have you learned from her?"

"Not a lot, but then, I haven't pushed. I am just happy to see her. She seems so shaken that she doesn't want to say much. I've put her to bed."

"Has she been harmed?"

"Not physically, at least as far as I can tell," Lily said.

"Good. Well, Wolfe won't get his fee for finding her, but that is really not important right now. He will want to see her, of course."

"Why? Hasn't she been through enough?"

"That certainly seems to be the case. But there is also a murder to be dealt with."

"But that is hardly Nero Wolfe's affair, is it?"

"I happen to think it is," came a voice from a doorway across the foyer. I spun around and saw Maureen Carr, clad in a bathrobe and slippers and with tousled hair and tired eyes. "I want to hire Mr. Wolfe to find out who killed Everett," she said.

"I thought you were asleep," Lily said in a voice that bordered on accusatory. "Right now, what you need is rest more than anything."

"The doorbell woke me up, and I'm glad it did. I can't be lazing around right now. I want to see Mr. Wolfe."

"Hold on," I told her. "Let's not rush things. I agree with Lily that you need time to . . . well, recuperate."

"Recuperate from *what*!" she snapped, hands on hips. "I appreciate the concern from both of you, but I do not have a need to be babied. You may have noticed that I am a big girl."

"Oh, I noticed that a long time ago," I said with a smile that I hoped would defuse what threatened to become a tense situation.

That brought the hint of a smile in return from Maureen. "I really do want to see Wolfe," she said. "And I overheard you tell Lily that your boss will want to see me."

"You heard correctly," I told her. "But the best way to handle this is for me to talk to him first. You have got to trust me on this."

"Lily has said so much about you over the years—all of it nice—that I do trust you, Archie."

"Ooh, I do wish you hadn't said that, Maureen," Lily put in. "Now he will be even more difficult to live with than he already was."

"Hey, my middle name is 'cordial' and 'unassuming.'"

Lily narrowed her eyes as she always does when giving me grief. "That's two middle names, Buster."

"Okay, I'm not about to argue the point. But I do need to talk to Mr. Wolfe before we move ahead," I said, turning to Maureen. "I promise that you will hear from me before the end of the day. You will be here, I trust."

"She will be here," Lily said. "I can guarantee it."

"That is plenty good enough for me," I replied as I got smiles from two very attractive women.

When I got home, Wolfe was at his desk, going through the morning mail, which Fritz had stacked on his blotter in my absence. He gave me a questioning look.

"She was at Lily's, of course."

"Of course."

"She is somewhat frazzled, which should hardly be a surprise, but she definitely is not unhinged, which means you won't be dealing with a hysterical female when she comes to call."

"That is comforting to know. When can you have her here?"

"When do you want her?"

"After lunch, at two forty-five. We are having baked scallops in shells," Wolfe announced, rising and heading for the dining room. All talk of business had ended until the meal was consumed.

# CHAPTER 23

After all that Maureen Carr had apparently been through, I was not about to have her travel from Lily's to the brownstone on West Thirty-Fifth without an armed escort. So, after finishing lunch and calling Lily to set things up, I slipped the Marley .38 into my shoulder holster and grabbed a cab to East Sixty-Ninth Street.

As I entered the penthouse for the second time that day, I saw that Maureen was ready to go—and so was Lily Rowan. I started to say something, but Lily cut me off before I could start.

"Maureen wants me with her, and I cannot imagine that Nero Wolfe would mind in the least," she said in a tone I know all too well—one that brooks no objections.

"Okay with me," I said, holding up both palms in surrender. "Although Wolfe may send you up to the plant rooms to gaze at his orchids. He knows how much you like them."

"I would really like it if Lily stayed with me," Maureen said. "I have never met Nero Wolfe, and I've heard that he can be intimidating."

"He's a pussycat," I said, which drew a laugh from Lily.

"Pussycat, eh?" she said. "I can only imagine how he would react if he heard you call him that."

"All right, maybe I misspoke just a tad. But, Maureen, you have nothing whatever to be afraid of from Nero Wolfe. Like me, he is pleased that you have been located."

When we got to the brownstone, Fritz opened the door, bowing as the two women entered. When their backs were to him, I noticed he was slyly admiring two pairs of legs.

Wolfe, who was at his desk, stood when we entered the office. Lily, knowing how unusual that is, looked at me with wide eyes. But of course, Maureen didn't realize what a break in tradition this was. I gestured our guest to the red leather chair, while Lily sat in a yellow one and I parked at my desk. Wolfe did not seem to be bothered in the least by Lily's presence. He probably was expecting it.

"Miss Carr," Wolfe said, "you have stories to tell, I am sure, but before we move on, I must inform you, if Miss Rowan has not already, that I was hired to locate you."

"Yes, she has told me you were hired by Lily and by Eric Mason," Maureen said, her voice strong. No cases of nerves.

"But of course, I cannot claim my fee, as it was not my doing, but rather circumstances, that conspired to locate you."

"Understood, and I am sorry to deprive you of your fee. But I have a proposition for you."

"Is that so?"

"I want you to find whoever it was that killed my brother, and I have heard that you charge high rates. I am fully capable of meeting those rates, Mr. Wolfe."

"We can discuss specific arrangements in due time. First, I would like a summary of your activities over the last few weeks."

I could give you a detailed report on Wolfe's conversation with Maureen Carr, but since you are going to hear much of it later on, I will not put you through having to read a lot of the same material twice.

"Do you plan to return to your residence, madam?"

"Eventually I will, of course. But for now, Lily has graciously allowed me to stay with her. After we leave here, we are going to my place to pick up some clothes. I have been living out of a suitcase long enough."

"Understood. Mr. Goodwin will accompany you in that endeavor. Do you have any thoughts as to who shot your brother?"

"Nothing definite. I assume the police have been investigating."

"They have, and without any apparent success."

"I was quite serious when I said I want to hire you to do the job," Maureen said, tight-lipped.

"I took it that you were serious," Wolfe said. "We will talk further. For now, I assume you are in need of rest."

"I hope that does not show too much," Maureen responded, brushing errant wisps of hair from her forehead. "About Everett: I realize that I should be devastated by his death, but the truth is, we never were at all close. As I'm sure you are aware, we were only half-siblings, many years apart in age, and we spent almost no time together. If that makes me sound coldhearted, I am sorry, but I'm only being candid."

"As Alexander Pope wrote in *Essay on Man*, 'be candid where we can,' and I for one appreciate candor," Wolfe said. "It avoids so-called niceties that too often interfere with free and open exchanges of thoughts and ideas. Now if you will excuse me, I have another appointment," he said, rising and walking out of the office.

Maureen wore a surprised look, but I jumped in before she started to speak. "Mr. Wolfe was not upset with you. It is just that he can be rather . . . abrupt. It's in his nature."

"I think she realizes that, Archie," Lily said. "I have been prepping her on what to expect from him. And what we just saw can only be described as vintage Nero Wolfe."

"Well said," I remarked. "There has been enough taxi riding recently. I have nominated myself as chauffeur, and like fugitives, we are about to leave the brownstone via the back way. You never know who might be watching the brownstone."

They both wore puzzled looks as we walked through the kitchen as Fritz and Wolfe were conferring about how the lamb should be cooked. They ignored us as we left by the door, went down the steps, and walked along a narrow path to a gate in the wooden fence that encloses the backyard.

"In all the years that I have known you, I have never been shown this," Lily remarked to me. "I begin to feel like a fugitive."

"You ain't seen nothin' yet, ladies," I told them as I opened the gate, which locks on the inside and cannot be accessed from the outside. Another narrow path between two buildings led to a sidewalk near the corner of Thirty-Fourth Street and Tenth Avenue.

"You both have just navigated the emergency exit route from the brownstone that Mr. Wolfe and I, as well as some of our freelance operatives, have used during crucial times to avoid visitors, often members of the constabulary, who were trying to batter down our door."

"In case you didn't know, he means the police," Lily said to Maureen, winking.

"Yeah, I did guess that. You must live an exciting life, Archie."

"So says the woman who has had plenty of excitement herself recently. Well, here we are."

"Curran Motors," Lily said, looking up at a sign on the front of a brick one-story garage.

"Yep, the secret is out. This is where we keep our cars, have for years," I said as we walked in.

"Hey, Archie," called out a guy in gray coveralls who had a rag sticking out of a pocket. "I assume you're here for the Heron. This isn't convertible weather, not yet. Maybe in a couple weeks, huh?"

"Hi, Art. Yes, I'm here for the Heron this time. Can I trust you to produce said automobile from wherever it's been stowed?"

"I will get it right away," he said, and within three minutes, Art pulled the sedan up in front of us. As he got out, he threw a lopsided grin at Lily and Maureen, and then said to me, "How come some guys have two beautiful women with them, and I don't have any?"

"Art, it's an intangible aura that I happen to have, and I wish I could explain it, but I can't. Call it the luck of the draw."

Both women climbed into the back seat and I gave Art a salute. "If I had a chauffeur's hat, I'd be wearing it," I told him as I pulled away.

"Sorry," I said, turning to the ladies. "I would rather be driving you in the convertible, but Art is right. This isn't the weather for it."

"He seemed kind of cute," Maureen remarked. "Too bad he doesn't have a girl."

"Hah, don't let Art fool you. He doesn't have a girl because he has a wife, and a damned nice-looking one, too. Along with two kids."

"Enough of this idle chatter," Lily said. "Onward, Jeeves."

I dropped the women off at Maureen's Park Avenue palace and idled at the curb while they went upstairs to gather some of her clothes. The doorman, Seamus, strode up to the Heron wearing his big, toothy Irish grin and said, "Hello, Mr. Goodwin. It is so nice to see Miss Carr back again. She has been away for some time now."

"She has, and I suspect she will be in and out for a while, but I agree that it's good that she has returned." I jawed with Seamus about such topics as the weather and the Giants' chances of getting into the World Series for close to a half hour. When the ladies finally came down, they were carrying a pair of suitcases and several dresses on hangers in zippered bags.

"How long before you have to come back here and replenish your wardrobe?" I asked Maureen.

"Oh, just ignore him," Lily countered. "Men love to see us looking nice, but they never appreciate how hard we work to please them."

My answer was a sigh as I pulled away and drove to Lily's building, where, to show that I was not the churl Lily likes to make me out to be, I helped cart the clothes up to the penthouse. After bidding the women good-bye and getting hugs of thanks and even a kiss from Lily, I returned home.

# CHAPTER 24

When I walked into the office, I saw that Wolfe had returned from his afternoon session with the orchids and was leaning back at his desk as if asleep.

"I certainly hope I am not disturbing you," I said.

He opened his eyes, blinked at me, and sniffed. "I have procrastinated," he announced. "Call Miss Carr. I wish to speak to her."

I called Lily's number, and when she answered, I told her Nero Wolfe wanted words with Maureen. "Really? I will get her," Lily replied.

Wolfe picked up his phone, and I stayed on. "Miss Carr, you earlier said you wanted to hire me to name the killer of your brother. Is your offer still on the table?"

"It certainly is, Mr. Wolfe. And I assure you that you will not find me a difficult negotiator regarding fees."

"That can wait for a later discussion, madam. For me to proceed, I may request help of a nonfinancial nature."

"All you have to do is ask," Maureen replied, "and I will do whatever I can."

"Satisfactory. Expect to hear from Mr. Goodwin."

After we all hung up, I turned to Wolfe. "What did I miss?"

"Miss? Nothing significant I am aware of."

"When I was gone did you. . . ?"

"Did I *what*, Archie?" Wolfe snapped.

"Never mind." What I was about to ask him: *Did you do that lip trick of yours while I was gone?* (I was referring, of course, to when Wolfe was in the process of solving a case, he would go into some sort of trance and his lips world go out and in, out and in before he awoke with the solution.) I never brought the subject up later, and I suppose I will never find out what he was up to in my absence. I shifted gears. "What kind of help are you going to need from Maureen Carr?"

Wolfe pulled in air and exhaled. "I want her to use what persuasive powers she possesses to get Stanley and Sofia Jurek to the brownstone at a time to be determined. Also, I want you to do likewise regarding Miles Hirsch and his bodyguard, Harley Everts."

"An interesting challenge. This begins to sound suspiciously like what Inspector Cramer refers to as one of your seances. Who else needs to be roped in?"

"Miss Rowan and Eric Mason, our former clients. By the way, it is possible Mr. Mason does not know that Miss Carr has returned."

"He probably isn't aware of it, unless Maureen herself has informed him. Okay, we know *who* you want present, now as to the *when*."

"Tomorrow night, nine o'clock," Wolfe said.

"Easy for you to say. When we make our calls, do we tell the invitees the purpose of the meeting?"

"The naming of Everett Carr's murderer."

I was not surprised. "And I suppose you will want Cramer present as well."

"I will personally offer him the opportunity to attend."

"Any suggestions on what I can use as bait to get Hirsch and his thug to make an appearance?"

"Over the years, I have been impressed by your persuasive powers. Bring those powers into play once again."

"All right, next question: Are you going to give Maureen Carr her assignment, or do you expect me to?"

"You always have had a good understanding of young women and how they think."

"Hah! You are giving me far too much credit. But I see that I have been given yet another task." Wolfe's response was to open an orchid catalog that had arrived in the morning mail. There was to be no further discussion, as is so often the case.

I figured I might as well start on the hardest task first, and I was hardly surprised to find that Miles Hirsch was not listed in the Manhattan phone directory. That meant a call to Lon Cohen.

"Yeah?" he answered after a couple of rings.

"I need some information," I told him.

"I'll try to mask my surprise. What is it this time?"

"Hey, don't get all uppity," I told him. "There may be a scoop here for you."

"Talk is cheap, Archie. What is it you need?"

"An unlisted phone number. And I believe you have the resources at your mighty journal to accommodate me."

"Flattery won't get you anywhere. Give me the name."

"Miles Hirsch."

"Why am I not shocked? The very same fellow you had me pull the clips on. Now I really do begin to smell a scoop."

"Stop salivating. Can you get me his phone number?"

"I'll call you back—soon," Lon said and hung up.

"Soon" turned out to be ten minutes, and Lon fed me the number. "Just remember who your friends are," he said.

"How can I forget, as often as you keep reminding me?"

I dialed the number Lon had given me, and the call was answered by a male in what seemed to be an English accent, or some approximation. "Mr. Hirsch's residence," he intoned.

"I would like to speak to Miles Hirsch," I said after getting the standard who-may-I-ask-is-calling response and giving my name.

There was silence on the line for close to a half minute, and then the English voice was back. "I am so sorry, sir, but Mr. Hirsch is indisposed."

"Oh dear, I'm sorry as well. I do hope it is nothing serious. Please tell Mr. Hirsch that we were so hoping he might be able to attend an important meeting at Mr. Nero Wolfe's residence at nine o'clock tomorrow night. It promises to be very important to Mr. Hirsch's business interests, and to his standing in the community."

Another silence, this time shorter. "Goddamn it, Goodwin, just what are you trying to pull? And how did you get this number?" Hirsch shouted as I jerked the receiver away from my ear.

"Pull? I am not sure what you mean, Mr. Hirsch. Mr. Wolfe was concerned that you might regret missing a gathering at his home that could affect your future."

"Now listen to me, and listen good, you two-bit private peeper. Nobody, and I mean nobody, tells me where I've got to be and when. You got that?"

"I certainly do, Mr. Hirsch. Mr. Wolfe will be sorry for your absence, as will Police Inspector Cramer, who I understand was looking forward to meeting you."

"Cramer? What the hell would he be doing at Wolfe's place? What kind of a racket are you guys pulling?"

"No racket at all, Mr. Hirsch. Nero Wolfe is a licensed private investigator in the state of New York."

That got a scornful laugh from Hirsch. "Hell, those clowns up in Albany will give a license to anybody as long as it brings dough into the state's coffers."

"You sound rather cynical," I remarked.

"Damn right. I've got reason to be with all that I've seen through the years."

"Interesting. I heard a similar reaction from a policeman recently," I told him. "It seems like a shame for you to miss out on this meeting," I remarked. "You may know several other people who will be present."

"Yeah, like who?"

"I am not at liberty to say at the moment."

"What a crock. Tell you what, Goodwin, I'm going to call Wolfe's bluff and show up tomorrow, and whether you guys like it or not, I'm going to bring Harley Everts along to watch my back."

"That's an excellent idea, Mr. Hirsch. I was going to suggest it myself, but you beat me to it."

My comment seemed to give the gambler pause, at least for a few seconds. He recovered and muttered something about seeing us tomorrow before hanging up. Next, I called one of my favorite numbers, and Lily answered.

"Is all well with Maureen?" I asked.

"Yes, she is still in recovery mode after all her adventures."

"I'm not surprised. Two items: One, has she talked to Mason since her . . . reemergence? And two, I need to speak to her."

"No, she hasn't called Mason; and she's resting, but she's not asleep. I'll get her."

"Hi, Archie," Maureen said after stifling a yawn. "Lily said that you needed to talk to me."

"First, I hope you're getting plenty of rest."

"Don't worry about that. Lily has been spoiling me."

"Glad to hear it. Mr. Wolfe has an assignment for you."

"Uh-oh, should I be worried?"

"I hardly think so. He is having a meeting tomorrow night at nine p.m. at his home, and we're in the process of gathering the attendees. He has asked that you invite Sofia and Stan Jurek."

"What's the meeting about, Archie?"

"Mr. Wolfe wants to learn more about how your brother happened to be shot. And after all, you are his client."

"I'm not sure what I should tell Sofia and Stan. I do know how upset they are—especially Sofia—for what I've been through and for what happened to Everett."

"Understood. Just tell them you have hired Mr. Wolfe to help you, and that one or the other of them may have some thoughts about anyone they knew or have seen who could help in his investigation."

"All right, I will telephone them. Should I get back to you with what they say?"

"Absolutely, and as quickly as possible. Mr. Wolfe really does feel they might be of some help. It is important you stress that to each of them."

"Aye, aye, sir."

"Two more things, Maureen: Bring Lily with you tomorrow night. And I know you haven't talked to Eric Mason, but we will want to invite him as well, being that he was a client. Do you have a problem with us asking that he come?"

"No . . . no, but won't he be surprised to see me, and get angry that I haven't called him?"

"That's possible, of course, but you can always say that you've been so traumatized that you've been in seclusion."

"Sounds pretty dramatic," Maureen said.

"Well, there has been plenty of drama lately. I hope to hear from you soon regarding the Jureks. By the way, do you have Mason's home number? We have been calling him at the ad agency."

She gave it to me, and after we signed off, I turned to Wolfe, who still had his nose in that orchid catalog. "You probably got the drift from hearing my end of those calls that Hirsch and his henchman are coming tomorrow night and Maureen will try to get the Jurek couple to show up."

"Do you doubt her success?"

"No, but if she does happen to strike out, I will exert my persuasive powers with them. I assume you want me to call Eric Mason."

"Your assumption is correct. Before you speak to him, I need to talk to Inspector Cramer."

Which translates to, *You call him, right now.* Like so many other numbers, I know the inspector's by heart. I dialed and after two rings got "Cramer!" shouted at me. He and Wolfe must have attended the same school of telephone etiquette. I nodded to my boss, who picked up his receiver.

"Good day, Inspector," he said.

"I haven't seen anything good about it yet," Cramer snapped. "And now with you on the line, it's only bound to get worse."

"You have not heard me out, sir. It's possible I have good news."

"I will be the judge of that."

"Very well. I have invited several people to the brownstone tomorrow night at nine. I plan to identify Everett Carr's murderer, who will be among those present, and I felt you might want to be on hand."

There was a long pause, which could have meant Cramer was gnawing on a stogie either in anger or in frustration. Finally, he found his voice, and it had an edge. "I was right; the day *has* gotten worse. Who are you going to finger?"

"You know better than to ask that, Mr. Cramer. There must be a full explanation before there can be a revelation."

"You sure can spit out the long words, Wolfe," he snarled. "So, it's to be another one of your goddamn spectacles. You should have gone on the stage. Broadway lost one of the great dramatic actors when you became a detective."

"Sarcasm does not become you, sir. Do you plan to be in attendance tomorrow night?"

"Yes, along with Sergeant Stebbins, whether you like it or not."

"I have no objection to his presence. In fact, I believe it to be a prudent move."

"Well, I am sure glad that I have your approval," Cramer said, hanging up.

"So that much is settled," I told Wolfe. "Now I'll call Eric Mason." That got a nod, nothing more.

"I wasn't sure I'd find you in," I told the ad man when he answered.

"And why not?" he said sharply. "I was beginning to wonder if I would ever hear from you or Nero Wolfe again. What's going on with the search for Maureen?"

"We have some news, but I can't tell you about it right now. There is going to be a gathering at Mr. Wolfe's brownstone tomorrow night, and you're invited."

"Why all the mystery? What the hell is going on?"

"You will find out at that time. Sorry, but Nero Wolfe does things his way. And he gets results."

Mason continued to grumble about how he's been in the dark for so long. I listened for a while to show I was sympathetic, but then told him I had other people to call and curtly ended the conversation.

No sooner had I hung up than the phone jangled. It was Maureen. "Archie, both of the Jureks will be at your place tomorrow night, although persuading them to come was not easy."

"Tell me about it."

"Sofia answered my call, and after I explained about the meeting, she seemed uneasy, saying she didn't understand why they should have to be at your place tomorrow. Then Stan came on the line and started barking at me. He said he was tired of being accused of things. I told him nobody was accusing him of anything, and that Mr. Wolfe just needed to learn more about my brother.

"Stan finally calmed down—he has quite a temper—and then he persuaded Sofia that it would be all right if they went to the meeting. She finally agreed, but not until they had talked for several minutes. I could hear the conversation through the receiver, and there was some whining on Sofia's part. She does not like confrontation of any kind, as I learned when she worked for me. It's a shyness that she's never gotten over."

"Congratulations on pulling it off. Now I can tell you something: Eric Mason also will be present tomorrow night. He was angry that we hadn't been in touch with him for a few days, and I heard him out and let him vent. I did not tell him you would be present, so be prepared for a reaction."

"I will steel myself," she said.

"I'm sure you will. Come a little early tomorrow night. It would be good if you were already seated when the others arrive."

# CHAPTER 25

So we were set for tomorrow's festivities. As usual, I had not caught up with Wolfe and his reasoning, although I had begun to have suspicions. He told me to make sure Saul Panzer would be present to welcome the guests and to serve drinks.

The next day dragged by as they always do when Wolfe is going to stage one of his show-and-tell sessions. I found a variety of ways to pass the time, including bringing the expense ledger up to date and making sure several bills got paid on time.

After a dinner in which Wolfe expounded on the generally positive impact immigration had made on American society in general, I set up the chairs in the office while Saul stocked the beverage cart with a variety of liquors and filled the ice bucket.

At eight thirty, Lily and Maureen arrived, each of them clearly on edge. "Because you are now the client, you get the place of honor, the red leather chair," I told Maureen, who did not appear to be overly impressed. Then I turned to Lily. "And for you, this chair in the front row—the farthest from me, I'm sorry to say, but that's how Mr. Wolfe wants it."

"He probably thinks if I sit close to you, we will murmur sweet nothings to each other, and I don't have to tell you how he feels about scenes like that."

"We will just have to do our murmurings some other time. I can wait if you can."

"It will be difficult," Lily said, "but then, I've got a lot of will-power. Who will be sitting with me in this row?"

"Miles Hirsch, the gambler, and next to you, his bodyguard, Harley Everts."

"Oh swell. Maybe I can strike up a conversation with this Everts about the brand of brass knuckles he uses."

"Now don't you go getting all sarcastic on me," I told Lily.

"Me, sarcastic, never, my dear. I prefer to call myself a realist."

"If I can interrupt this snappy patter, Archie," Maureen said, "as the client, I would like to know the rest of the seating arrangements."

"You certainly are entitled to that. The second row will have Stan Jurek closest to me, then Sofia and Eric Mason. And the two chairs in the back will be occupied by Inspector Cramer and his sergeant, Purley Stebbins. Oh, and Saul Panzer will be parked on the sofa against the wall as an onlooker."

No sooner had I got those words out than the bell sounded, which sent Fritz to the front door. Seconds later, followed by the heavy-footed Stebbins, Cramer stepped in, looked around, noted the presence of Lily, Maureen, and Panzer, and scowled. "Miss Rowan, I have known you since you were a child, and as you are aware, I knew and respected your father—a fine man, and one who helped me early in my career. I can only guess how he would feel if he knew you were a party to these Wolfe-Goodwin shenanigans."

"Oh, I think he would be just fine with them, Inspector, just like he was fine nurturing your career back when you were pounding the beat." Cramer made a face but did not respond.

"And, Inspector," Lily continued, "this is Maureen Carr, a very good friend of mine who is here to learn who killed her brother."

Before Cramer could respond, the bell chimed again, and the Jureks came into the office, looking around nervously. They were followed immediately by Eric Mason, whose expression when he saw Maureen was one for the ages. His face went from shock to pleasure to anger in matter of seconds. "Why . . . you are . . . how. . . ?"

To prevent the man from becoming a babbling idiot, Maureen quietly said, "We will talk later, Eric. Now is not the time."

That shut him up, and he plopped down where I directed as the Jureks also sat without complaint and without uttering a word.

The next, and last, sounding of the doorbell brought Miles Hirsch and his sidekick Everts in, each of them looking like he would rather be anywhere else.

I got the pair seated in the front row. Hirsch started to speak, but he was interrupted by the arrival of Wolfe, who detoured around his desk and got seated. He surveyed the gathering and spoke each person's name, ending with Cramer and Stebbins.

"What the hell are those two doing here?" Hirsch demanded as he looked over his shoulder and jabbed a gnarled finger at two of New York's Finest. "You got the cops in your pocket?" he demanded of Wolfe.

"Shut up, or we'll shut you up!" Cramer barked. "We are here as observers right now, although more outbursts from you might alter our role."

"Mr. Cramer is correct that he and Sergeant Stebbins are here as observers, and they are present at my invitation and remain at my sufferance. Do you have any further questions, Mr. Hirsch?"

The gambler folded his arms across his chest and shook his head.

"Good, now if we may continue, I am going to have beer," Wolfe said, pressing the buzzer in the leg-hole of his desk. "Would anyone else like something to drink? We have a well-stocked bar."

"I didn't realize this was to be a cocktail party," Mason huffed, apparently still sore at Maureen for not having communicated with him.

"I'll have some of Wolfe's hootch like I did one other time here. Give me that good scotch again," Hirsch said. "With a dash of water—and I mean only a dash."

"Me, too," grunted Everts.

"Oh, what the hell, I'll play along," Mason said. "Make mine a rye on the rocks."

Wolfe nodded to Saul, who rose from his perch on the sofa, a tweed sports coat nicely hiding the S&W snub-nosed .38 nestled in his shoulder holster. He went to the bar cart and began preparing the drinks. After they had been delivered, Wolfe took a sip of the beer Fritz had brought in and again looked over the assemblage.

"I ask your patience, as we are dealing with a complex consecution."

"What the hell is a consecution?" Hirsch demanded.

"A sequence of events," Mason said irritably. "We had better not interrupt the man, or we may end up here all night."

"Thank you, sir," Wolfe said. "I will not keep any of you here longer than is necessary to explain the denouement."

"What is a denou—oh, never mind," Hirsch said. "This guy"—he gestured toward Mason—"is right. Can't we move this along? We've all got places to be, I'm sure."

"Let us then proceed," Wolfe said. "This all began as a missing persons case, and that individual is Maureen Carr, who is now, ironically, my client." Wolfe glanced in her direction. "I was hired by Lily Rowan and Eric Mason to locate Miss Carr, who had not been seen for days and who failed to appear at one or more social functions where she had been expected. She also had been absent from her own home for an extended period, which puzzled her housekeeper, Mrs. Jurek.

"Even with the help of Mr. Goodwin and other investigators I often employ, we were initially unsuccessful in locating our subject—that is, until through some dogged research we learned she had been up in the Albany area, dining with Mr. Hirsch."

"Now wait a minute, damn it, whose word do you have for that?" Miles Hirsch demanded, rising halfway out of his chair.

"Do you deny the occurrence, sir? Perhaps we should ask Miss Carr about that meal at a roadhouse north of Albany." Wolfe turned to Maureen.

"Yes, we did have lunch up there," she said. "I can name the place, if you'd like."

"Oh, now I get it," Hirsch said, "this has been a setup. You've brought her here to contradict everything I say. Her word against mine."

Wolfe ignored the gambler. "Miss Carr, how did you and Mr. Hirsch happen to meet and dine at that location upstate?"

"I was handing Mr. Hirsch a certified check for fifty thousand dollars."

"Indeed? For what purpose?"

"Now wait a minute—I feel like I'm on trial here!" Hirsch barked.

"Just to make something clear," Inspector Cramer cut in, "this is not a courtroom, whatever Nero Wolfe thinks, and you do not have to respond to any charges or comments." Cramer seemed to be coming to Hirsch's defense, although it was clear from the inspector's facial expression that he had little if any use for the gambler and horse breeder.

"Thank you for clarifying that," Wolfe said, glaring at Cramer. "Miss Carr, for what reason were you giving Mr. Hirsch that certified check?"

"I was paying off a debt for my brother, who had a gambling problem and had borrowed heavily from Mr. Hirsch."

"Are you in the habit of lending large sums of money to individuals who gamble?" Wolfe asked Hirsch.

"No comment."

Wolfe turned to Maureen. "Would you describe your brother as one who gambled heavily?"

She nodded. "I had never been close to Everett, but I always knew he had this problem, usually involving horse racing. I was unaware that he had lost such large sums until I got a telephone call from my brother." She looked at Hirsch. "This . . . person said Everett owed him thousands of dollars, and he wanted his money. Everett told me his tone was threatening."

"How did Mr. Hirsch select the Albany area as the place for your meeting?"

"He told me that at the time he was staying at his home in Saratoga Springs and that it was more convenient for him if we met up there. I did not feel like I had any choice in the matter."

"Did the two of you dine alone?"

"Yes, although when he picked me up at my hotel in Albany, he had a driver—that man," Maureen said, pointing a finger at Everts.

"It would seem that you function in a variety of roles for Mr. Hirsch," Wolfe stated. Everts shrugged but said nothing.

"After you returned from Albany," Wolfe said to Maureen, "you did not go back to your home but rather to the residence of a friend in Greenwich Village."

"Yes, I was trying to . . . well, go underground, I suppose you might say."

"For what purpose, madam?"

"I did not want to see Hirsch again."

"Had he threatened you?"

"When we had that lunch, he told me I might have to pay him more money, because Everett was running up more debts."

"With money Mr. Hirsch was supplying him?"

"I suppose so. I don't know where else Everett could have gotten it."

"Am I correct in assuming Mr. Hirsch charges interest on these loans?"

"Boy, does he ever! That's why, once he got hold of me, he did not want to let go," Maureen said, glaring at Hirsch, who seemed to be bored by the proceedings. I half expected him to start yawning.

"Unfortunately, you were not able to shake Mr. Hirsch by moving from your address to another one."

"Then you must know that he and this Everts came to the Greenwich Village house—Elaine Musgrove's—where Everett and I were staying. I had gotten the key from the man who looks after her place when she is away. Elaine, bless her, had wired him from France and asked him to give me the key after I had talked to her."

"How did Mr. Hirsch find you?"

"I really don't know, unless he followed me when I left home. I hadn't told anyone where I was going. I was frankly terrified."

"What did Mr. Hirsch say to you when he came to your temporary abode?"

"To start with, he fooled me by having this Everts man ring the bell, and when I answered on the speaker, he said 'Western Union.' I did not recognize his voice, so I opened the door and they both pushed on in. Then Hirsch laughed and said something like 'So you thought you would lose me by ducking out, eh? Well, Harley and I, we want to keep close track of you. We never know when we might need you.'"

"How did your brother happen to be in that Greenwich Village home with you?" Wolfe asked.

"Everett had called me at home in a panic and wanted me to help keep him from this . . . Hirsch. So that's how we both ended up staying at Elaine's house for a day or so, and when these two men came barging in, Everett went out the back way, so they never saw him. I never saw him again, either," Maureen said in a somber tone.

"When I found out what had happened to him—the shooting was all over Greenwich Village, as you can imagine—I panicked again and left the Greenwich Village house by the back door so as not to be seen in case Hirsch was watching the place. I stayed with Sofia and Stanley for a couple of nights and then called Lily, who took me in."

"Miss Carr, who do you think killed your brother?" Wolfe asked.

"Don't try to pin this on me, damn it," Hirsch interrupted. "Why would I want to get rid of someone who owed me money? That makes no sense."

Once again, Wolfe ignored Hirsch, giving Maureen a questioning look.

"I really have no idea who did it. I saw so little of Everett that I don't know anything about who his friends were—or his enemies, assuming that he had some enemies, given what happened."

"Mr. Jurek, did you know Everett Carr?" Wolfe asked.

Stan Jurek flinched, surprised by being brought into the conversation. "Uh, well, I had met him, but I can't say that I really knew the man."

"What were the circumstances of your having met?"

"We both, well . . . we like to bet on the horses. We ran into each other in a . . . a bookie joint."

"Would you say you were successful in your wagering endeavors?"

Jurek hunched his shoulders. "Well, I've had some good days and some not-so-good days."

"You must have learned during your conversations that Mr. Carr was related to your wife's employer."

"Yeah, you know, we did. What a coincidence in a city this large, huh? We laughed about it, although I got the impression that the Carrs weren't very close."

"From our earlier conversation, I learned that you saw a lot of action during the war, and that you killed a German soldier in hand-to-hand combat," Wolfe said.

"I did," San Jurek replied. "It was either him or me."

"Did you, like so many servicemen, bring home any souvenirs from Europe?"

"Oh, a few," Jurek said offhandedly. "An iron cross and some medals off a Jerry corpse I came across, and the Luger from the guy I shot."

"The spoils of war," Wolfe observed, turning to Sofia. "And you, madam, were most generous in giving Miss Carr a place to stay during a time of turmoil for her."

Sofia's face reddened. "Stan and I were happy to do that. She was so frightened."

"I understand that after she had stayed in your apartment and Mr. Jurek left for work, the two of you took a taxi to a bank. I am most interested in that occurrence."

Sofia looked down at her lap and kneaded her hands. "I had asked her for some money," she said hoarsely.

Wolfe nodded. "No doubt you were somewhat strapped financially, not having worked for Miss Carr for several weeks."

"Yes, yes, that is it," Sofia said.

"What you're saying is that my salary isn't big enough, is that it?" Stan Jurek demanded.

"Miss Carr, may I inquire as to how much money you gave to your housekeeper that day?" Wolfe asked.

"I was hoping this wouldn't come up," Maureen replied in a subdued tone. "I withdrew five thousand dollars on our trip to the bank."

"What!" It was Jurek. "We're not broke, that's just plain charity," he said sharply to his wife.

"How dire is your situation?" Wolfe asked Sofia.

"Pretty bad," she said, again in a soft voice.

"Because of your husband's gambling?"

"Now wait a minute! We did not come in here so that you could air our dirty linen in public," Jurek said, standing as if to leave.

"Sit down!" Cramer spat. "Nobody leaves until I say so."

"Oh, so this really is your party, after all," Hirsch said, "despite Wolfe's claim that you and your sergeant are just here as observers. What a lot of hooey!"

"Perhaps Inspector Cramer misspoke," Wolfe said in a conciliatory tone. "Mr. Jurek, you mentioned that among the items you brought back from the war is a Luger pistol."

"Yes, and it's a dandy," he said, having calmed down a bit and being happy to talk about his military exploits. "I've thought about putting it in a glass case, along with the iron cross and the medals I took off the guy's uniform. Kind of like trophies."

"But you have never fired the weapon?" Wolfe asked.

"Hell no, although the bullets are still in it."

"Mr. Carr was killed by a weapon that fired nine-millimeter shells, the caliber used in a Luger," Wolfe said.

"I suppose there are lots of Lugers around," Jurek said. "What are you trying to say?"

"I am simply making an observation, sir. Mrs. Jurek, did you ever have occasion to meet Mr. Carr?"

Sofia stiffened. "I . . . do not believe so."

"But you knew who he was?"

"Oh yes, Stan had mentioned him to me."

"Did they meet often?"

"I don't know that."

"And you are sure you have never met Mr. Carr?" Wolfe repeated his earlier question.

"I . . . I . . ." Sofia began to sniffle.

"Let me suggest this scenario, madam. You have indeed met Everett Carr. You felt the man was a bad influence upon your husband by encouraging his gambling on the horses, a habit that has wreaked havoc on your family's finances."

"Stop this!" Stan Jurek shouted. "I will not let—"

"Mr. Jurek, if you are unable to control yourself, I will ask Mr. Goodwin and Mr. Panzer to forcibly relocate you to the front room until I have concluded," Wolfe said. Jurek had been hyperventilating, and after Wolfe's threat, he slowly returned to normal breathing.

"To continue with my scenario, madam, you contrived to meet Mr. Carr—I will leave it to the police to determine how that was accomplished—and the two of you met in a passage-way between buildings in Greenwich Village. You of course knew about your husband's prized Luger, and you took it with you to the rendezvous.

"Your plan was to insist that Mr. Carr stop meeting your husband and abetting his gambling proclivities. You planned to threaten him with the Luger to underscore the seriousness of your demand. But—"

"Please!" This time, it was Sofia who interrupted. "Please, that is enough. You are right, you are right, I did have the gun in my hand, but I just wanted to use it to, to threaten him. But do you know what that man did? He laughed at me, and he grabbed for the gun. He said, 'What is a tiny little lady like you doing with such a big, bad weapon? You are nothing but a silly goose.' That is what he called me—a silly goose! We wrestled for the gun, and at that moment, I hated him even more than before. I tried to pull the gun back as he kept holding on to it, and it . . . it fired and fired. He fell . . ."

She broke down and started sobbing as her husband cradled her head in his lap. Tears rolled down his cheeks as well.

Wolfe, who can't stand scenes like the one that was unfolding before him, got up and walked out of the office.

For the first several seconds after Wolfe departed, there was what I could only term stunned silence. The lone sounds were the muffled crying of Sofia Jurek and the muttering of her husband.

Finally, Inspector Cramer spoke. "Purley, call headquarters and ask them to bring a policewoman here—and right now!" Stebbins looked questioningly at me, and I nodded in the direction of my desk, a signal of tacit permission for him to use my phone. Despite the differences Purley and I have had over the years, and they have been doozies, sometimes our hostilities must be suspended. This was one of those times.

Lily came over to Maureen and put an arm on her shoulder, then whispered something in her ear. Miles Hirsch and

Harley Everts rose, and, wearing a sneer, Hirsch looked around and said to Cramer, "Bet you thought you were going to get me tonight, didn't you? Sorry I had to spoil your evening, copper."

"Be smug while you still can," the inspector retorted as the gambler walked out. "Your day will come."

Stebbins finished his call and, shaking his head, he looked down at the Jureks, who were still clinging to each other. Eric Mason came over to Maureen, and the two of them repaired to the sofa and huddled in a conversation that I made no attempt to eavesdrop on.

Lily came and stood with me, saying, "I thought Mr. Wolfe was pretty hard on Sofia, didn't you?"

"It was not fun to watch, for sure. But then, Sofia was pretty hard on Everett Carr as well," I said.

"But she was trying to protect her husband."

"I will grant you that, and I suppose that eventually it will be up to a jury to decide her fate. Now if you will excuse me, my dear. I must make a call to Lon Cohen at the *Gazette*, who may very well be expecting to hear from me. He will, of course, call Inspector Cramer and be able to scoop the competition when his early edition comes out around midday tomorrow. He will love the fact that it is now too late for the morning papers like the *Times* and *Daily News* to get anything into print tonight. And most important, Lon will be in Nero Wolfe's debt, at least for a while."

# CHAPTER 26

The case against Sofia Jurek ended up generating lots of headlines and photographs. First for the murder itself, of course, but then for the trials—plural. For many of the courtroom reporters, Sofia became a tragic figure, one who had been driven to violence by forces beyond her control and who was seen by some to be an accidental murderess.

Gambling took center stage at her first trial, with some social reformers demanding that parimutuel horse racing be banned in New York State because of the harm it does to working families. For good or ill, that campaign got nowhere.

The district attorney's office had first planned to charge Sofia with first-degree murder, but they decided premeditation would be too hard to prove, so they went to a second-degree charge. Sofia was represented by one of the best trial lawyers in the city. He was hired by Maureen Carr—despite the defendant having killed Maureen's brother.

The courtroom drama garnered plenty of coverage, on the radio and in magazines as well as in print. However, the trial was aborted when a reporter from Lon Cohen's *Gazette* discovered that one of the jurors was a recovering gambler—mainly on horse racing. A second trial is currently underway, and Lon has told me his reporters think this one could drag on for weeks, particularly with Sofia being portrayed as a martyr and a victim.

Inspector Cramer's "Your day will come" threat to Miles Hirsch came to pass a little over a week ago when the gambler and horse breeder was charged with the doping of one of his own horses in a race at a track in Florida. Lon is certain that Hirsch will go to trial, which could result in his being permanently banned from horse racing, to say nothing of a possible prison sentence.

As far as I am aware, nothing more has been heard from or about Hirsch's dubious sidekick, Harley Everts. Maybe the tough has found himself a new boss for whom he can perform questionable duties.

Maureen Carr and Eric Mason are still being seen together at various social events around town, although Lily Rowan tells me that the lady still cannot make up her mind about marrying the creative advertising ace. I don't have strong feelings on the subject one way or the other, and neither does Lily.

In case you are the type who likes to keep track of details, Maureen did indeed pay Nero Wolfe for solving the murder of her brother, and the fee Wolfe charged, forty thousand dollars, was acceptable to his deep-pocketed client. It was acceptable to me as well, because when Wolfe gets his fee and the bank balance gets an infusion, he is easier to put up with. I am all for a peaceful household, and on that topic, Fritz Brenner and Theodore Horstmann are in total agreement with me.

# AUTHOR NOTES

This story is set in the aftermath of World War II, when the United States was adjusting, not always easily, to peacetime after nearly four years of American conflict in Europe and the Pacific.

Among the places mentioned in the narrative is the William Sloane House YMCA, on West Thirty-Fourth Street near Ninth Avenue in Manhattan. The fourteen-story Sloan House, once said to be the largest residential Y in the country with sixteen hundred, was built in 1930, sold in 1963 for five million dollars, and later converted to rental apartments.

I stayed there on several occasions in 1961 when on weekend passes from my army post at Fort George G. Meade in Maryland. The rooms were spartan but clean and neat, and the price was right for a young GI. And those trips to New York gave me a wonderful opportunity to familiarize myself with the city that plays such a large part in these stories.

If present-day New Yorkers reading this narrative are puzzled to learn that long-distance passenger trains once departed from Grand Central Terminal, it should be noted that the historic station was for decades home to many famous intercity trains, including the Twentieth Century Limited, the Southwestern Limited, and the Commodore Vanderbilt. But in 1991, Amtrak consolidated all its New York passenger operations at Penn Station, and Grand Central became solely a commuter depot.

If the name Mortimer M. Hotchkiss, a vice president of the Continental Bank & Trust Co., strikes a familiar chord with readers, it is because Rex Stout also had used him as Nero Wolfe's banker. If you have found a good man, stick with him.

Four books have been of great help to me in my attempts to re-create the world of Nero Wolfe and the other characters and places Rex Stout created over four decades. They are: *Nero Wolfe of West Thirty-Fifth Street: The Life and Times of America's Largest Private Detective* by William S. Baring-Gould (The Viking Press, New York, 1968); *The Nero Wolfe Cookbook* by Rex Stout and the Editors of the Viking Press (Viking Press, New York, 1973); *The Brownstone House of Nero Wolfe* by Ken Darby as Told by Archie Goodwin (Little, Brown, Boston, 1983); and *Rex Stout: A Biography* by John McAleer (Little, Brown, Boston, 1977). The McAleer volume won an Edgar Award in the biography category from the Mystery Writers of America.

As with my previous Nero Wolfe books, I thank the estate of Rex Stout for graciously granting me permission to continue the adventures of Nero Wolfe, Archie Goodwin, and the other recurring characters who were so brilliantly created and depicted by Mr. Stout.

I also thank my agent, Martha Kaplan, as well as Otto Penzler and Charles Perry of Mysterious Press and the fine team at

Open Road Integrated Media, all of whom have supplied much-appreciated support and encouragement.

And I save my biggest thanks for my wife, Janet, who has been a partner in every aspect of my life for well over a half century.

# ABOUT THE AUTHOR

Robert Goldsborough is an American author best known for continuing Rex Stout's famous Nero Wolfe series. Born in Chicago, he attended Northwestern University and upon graduation went to work for the Associated Press, beginning a lifelong career in journalism that would include long periods at the *Chicago Tribune* and *Advertising Age*. While at the *Tribune*, Goldsborough began writing mysteries in the voice of Rex Stout, the creator of iconic sleuths Nero Wolfe and Archie Goodwin. Goldsborough's first novel starring Wolfe, *Murder in E Minor* (1986), was met with acclaim from both critics and devoted fans, winning a Nero Award from the Wolfe Pack.

# THE NERO WOLFE MYSTERIES

FROM MYSTERIOUSPRESS.COM
AND OPEN ROAD MEDIA

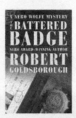

MYSTERIOUSPRESS.COM

Otto Penzler, owner of the Mysterious Bookshop in Manhattan, founded the Mysterious Press in 1975. Penzler quickly became known for his outstanding selection of mystery, crime, and suspense books, both from his imprint and in his store. The imprint was devoted to printing the best books in these genres, using fine paper and top dust-jacket artists, as well as offering many limited, signed editions.

Now the Mysterious Press has gone digital, publishing ebooks through **MysteriousPress.com**.

**MysteriousPress.com** offers readers essential noir and suspense fiction, hard-boiled crime novels, and the latest thrillers from both debut authors and mystery masters. Discover classics and new voices, all from one legendary source.

FIND OUT MORE AT

WWW.MYSTERIOUSPRESS.COM

FOLLOW US:

@emysteries and Facebook.com/MysteriousPressCom

MysteriousPress.com is one of a select group of publishing partners of Open Road Integrated Media, Inc.

**THE MYSTERIOUS BOOKSHOP**, founded in 1979, is located in Manhattan's Tribeca neighborhood. It is the oldest and largest mystery-specialty bookstore in America.

The shop stocks the finest selection of new mystery hardcovers, paperbacks, and periodicals. It also features a superb collection of signed modern first editions, rare and collectable works, and Sherlock Holmes titles. The bookshop issues a free monthly newsletter highlighting its book clubs, new releases, events, and recently acquired books.

58 Warren Street
info@mysteriousbookshop.com
(212) 587-1011
Monday through Saturday
11:00 a.m. to 7:00 p.m.

## FIND OUT MORE AT:

www.mysteriousbookshop.com

## FOLLOW US:

@TheMysterious and Facebook.com/MysteriousBookshop

OPEN ROAD

INTEGRATED MEDIA

Find a full list of our authors and
titles at www.openroadmedia.com

FOLLOW US
@OpenRoadMedia

CPSIA information can be obtained
at www.ICGtesting.com
Printed in the USA
JSHW020154090523
41449JS00002B/2